WOURISM
And Other Stories

Ian Whates

Wourism. *First published in Galaxy's Edge 10, 2014.*
Montpellier. *First published in Galaxy's Edge 19, 2016.*
No Smoke Without Fire. *First published in Fables from the Fountain (NewCon Press), 2011.*
For Your Own Good. (original to this collection)
Digital Democracy. *First published in The Human Genre Project (Edinburgh University), 2009.*
Eros for Annabelle. *First published in Nature, 2013.*
Reaper's Rose. *First published in Nightmare Magazine, 2016.*
Beth and Bones. *First published in Holdfast 5, 2015.*
Royal Flush. *First published in Escape Velocity 4, 2009.*
Triptych i) Browsing. *First published in Nature, 2016.*
Triptych ii) Trending. *First published in Daily Science Fiction, 2014.*
Triptych iii) Temporary Friends. (original to this collection)
The Failsafe. *First published in Explorations: Colony (Woodbridge Press), 2017.*
Sane Day. (original to this collection)
Between Blood and Bone. *First published in Daily Science Fiction, 2018.*
The Gun. *First published in Speculative Realms: Beneath the Surface (Speculative Realms Press), 2008.*
The Final Fable. *First published in 2001: An Odyssey in Words (NewCon Press), 2018.*

www.lunapresspublishing.com
ISBN-13: 978-1-911143-75-8

For Neil Williamson:
fine writer and true friend.

Contents

Wourism and Other Stories: An Introduction by Ian Whates

Short stories have always been important to me. Reading them as a young teen, in anthologies borrowed from the library, was my gateway to discovering so many of the authors whose work I would come to love. Writing them was the means by which I honed my craft and first learned how to create credible characters and mould an effective narrative. Before I ever dared to present a novel to publishers or agents, I had sold some two dozen short stories and seen them published in a variety of venues, and it was short fiction that brought me my first appearances on award shortlists.

The problem is that with every passing year time becomes an increasingly precious commodity. Novel contracts, novella commitments, and running a busy independent publisher, have combined to squeeze the available time from every direction, and writing short stories is one of the things that has suffered. Whereas once the goal of producing one short piece a month would have sounded perfectly reasonable, now I'm delighted if I manage one or two in a calendar year.

This volume represents virtually all my published stories from the past five years, along with two pieces I held back from previous collections due to the vague intention of including them one day in a mosaic novel (as explained further in the accompanying story notes at the back of this book), one which always felt incomplete if lifted from its original context in a shared world volume, until I wrote a follow up this year and so can now present both in one book, and a couple of new pieces that have never appeared anywhere before.

Therefore, the stories gathered here were written at different times for different reasons and were intended to achieve different things. As a result, they provide the variety that any such collection should boast – there's humour, dark forebodings, pointed social commentary and pure fun dotted around the pages. Yet gathering these disparate sparks of narrative into one place and viewing them as a single body of work reveals a few aspects that have surprised me, even though I wrote them. I hadn't realised until now, for example, how short much of my recent fiction has been. Yes, I knew that I'd written a number of flash pieces with specific purpose in mind (the three components of "A Triptych for Tomorrow" being prime examples) but hadn't appreciated how prevalent that brevity has been in the past few years. I suspect this is a product of the time pressure mentioned earlier. Ten years ago, a story idea may well have been allowed to evolve and expand at leisure, whereas now when an opportunity to write presents itself (or the urge to do so becomes too overwhelming to ignore), I tend to focus on producing as short and sharp a narrative as possible, because I'm conscious of the other twenty things I ought to be dealing with at the same time... Don't get me wrong, I'm not suggesting these pieces are rushed or under-cooked, merely that they are leaner, more focussed than once they might have been. This is by no means a bad thing, it just makes this volume a little different from previous ones; nor is this a collection of flash fiction. There are several stories here that comfortably top 4,000 words and more, but I was a little surprised by the number that don't.

Another aspect that caught me off guard was the number of stories told in the first person. This isn't a voice I've ever employed for a novel-length work, where a broader canvas has always felt more appropriate and more convenient, but it is a perspective that I feel comfortable in using for shorter fiction. It's a mechanism that can make the story more immediate and help to hold the reader close to the narrative. At a quick count, I've utilised first person for seven of the seventeen pieces in this book, which is a larger minority than I would have anticipated.

I'm very proud of the stories in *Wourism*. Every craftsman in whatever field likes to think that they improve at what they're doing, that with the benefit of experience – we never stop learning, after all – they are able to produce more polished, more refined work. I'm no different, and I feel that this volume includes some of my best and most effective short stories to date.

I can only hope that you agree.

Ian Whates
Cambridgeshire
December 2018

Wourism

"The storms were the worst thing. The power outages and food shortages, the ignominy of standing in queues for basics, even bread and water—we coped with all of that. This was war, after all. The constant fear of explosion and the almost incessant gunfire, the destruction of buildings and the roads—they were terrible, horrific, but it's amazing what you can learn to live with when you have to. The weather turning against us, though, that was the final straw. None of us had ever seen rain like it: relentless, pummelling the city as if God Herself had forsaken us and joined in the bombardment; and as for the lightning…"

The woman's narrative was abruptly punctuated by a loud peal of thunder and the pervading gloom shattered in a dazzle of electric discharge. Somebody, possibly Gretchen, exclaimed in surprise and even I started a little. This well-staged drama heralded the surround-sound arrival of steady rain and a rolling series of thunderous rumblings, though the latter were far more subdued than that first spectacular clap.

The woman continued speaking. The image of her narrow face still dominated the room, but now behind it and through it a distant cityscape began to emerge, illuminated by vivid lightning strikes and the ruddy stain of smouldering fires.

"This was the closest our collective spirit came to breaking," the woman said. "Even the deaths seemed so much worse in the relentless storms. Disposing of bodies became a logistical nightmare as well as an emotional one. Somebody claimed that the freak weather was a sign of severe damage to the ionosphere, that in a struggle somewhere high above us doomsday weapons were being deployed, unleashing fearsome energies that had unbalanced the atmosphere of the entire planet. Such things meant nothing to us. What did we care about the planet or even the next district over? Our whole world had narrowed down to a handful of streets and the struggle to survive for just one more day."

The woman's face faded. Perspective tilted and we swooped down towards the besieged city and then into it, stopping only once we had reached street level. The sound of rainfall intensified and it was joined by the chatter of small-arms fire and the clatter of running footsteps. The 3D effect was far more immediate and more convincing now that we were this close. There was even a faint smell of smoke and of dampness, and a billow of heat from a fire at our backs. Only the absence of any actual rain hampered the suspension of disbelief. Long shadows moved across the walls of shattered buildings to our left: people running. A man screamed, and one of the shadows convulsed in mid-stride, threw up its arms and collapsed.

The woman's face appeared once more, superimposed on the street scene to hover in the air before us. Her eyes held a great weariness that underlined her words. "Little Danilo, my younger brother, was killed in the first few days of the bombardment; my eldest, Toma, towards the end." She spoke with a cold detachment that made her account all the more chilling. "Toma had joined the militia by then. No one lived long in the militia. The imminence of his death overshadowed the start of each new day like a pall and haunted our dreams at night, until it became reality. My mother fell ill not long after. By this stage there was no medicine—supplies had run out months before. We did our best, but all we had to offer her were prayers and love and comforting words. She didn't leave her bed in the last two weeks and died the day before the cease-fire. My father never really recovered. Nor, in truth, did any of us."

A caption appeared beneath the woman's face: 'Jasna Petrović: Survivor', it read.

"My name is Jasna Petrović, and I was one of the lucky ones."

With that, she was gone. The soundtrack had dwindled to nothing during her final declaration and now the scene faded too as the lights came back up, to leave us blinking at each other across a plain-walled room.

In a gauche display that the word 'insensitive' didn't begin to cover, somebody beside me started clapping. I was mortified to realise that it was Alex.

"What?" he asked in the face of my glare. "It was a very good show."

"For fuck sake, Alex…" I don't swear as a rule, but he'd earned it.

I was eight months out of university and yet to decide what I wanted to do with my life. Alex was seven years older than me, worked in corporate finance for a company with offices on five worlds and had an apartment in the sort of complex my friends and I used to dream of seeing inside. He was big on team building and I would tease him that his favourite words were 'bonding' and 'incentive'.

As I looked around I noticed a middle-aged woman standing stock-still while everyone about her relaxed and chatted; an island of calm amidst the fidgeting. Tall, slender, she wore a burgundy suit—very smart and business-like—and was staring straight ahead, as if she could still see the harrowing scene long after the rest of us had lost it in the glare of brightened lights.

"Oh, come on, Ginny. She's not real, you know," Alex said, reclaiming my attention. "You do know that, don't you? Just an actress hired to play the part, and her performance was outstanding, so I showed my appreciation."

I wasn't so sure. The narrator's eyes and her voice—the whole presentation—seemed to resonate with sincerity to me. Of course, Alex would argue that it was meant to.

He turned away to talk to Gretchen and Hassan—a couple we'd fallen in with since arriving here. I consulted my wrist perminal. A quick search of the local database revealed that there had been no fewer than seven Jasna Petrovićs resident in Serna at the outbreak of the war. A flutter of fingertips brought a parade of images scrolling across the screen. I froze the sequence at one who *might* have been our narrator, though she was a lot younger when this was taken; and she was smiling, which was something she had never threatened to do during the presentation. I narrowed the search to images of this particular Jasna Petrović and took great satisfaction in discovering that yes, the woman was genuine.

Her story and her suffering were real, whatever Alex might think.

He could have checked all this easily enough on his own perminal had he wanted to. He wouldn't, of course; far too comfortable in his own false assumptions. Why risk undermining a declared cynicism with anything as inconvenient as the truth?

"If you'd like to follow me, ladies and gentlemen," Malcolm, our slick, camp, white-suited guide said, "we have some wartime armament to show you next; a unique collection of genuine artillery pieces and weaponry that saw service during the siege and were recovered and restored at the end of hostilities."

"Now we're talking," Alex said, flashing me a broad grin, taking it for granted that we two were collaborators in his enthusiasm.

He was soon chatting happily with Gretchen and Hassan. None of them seemed to notice that I lagged a little behind.

Everyone knew the basic story of this place; that while the rest of the city was rebuilt and reshaped in the aftermath of the war, one large section of Serna had been kept as a ruin—though it hadn't, of course; that was just the desired illusion. In fact this area too had been rebuilt, but in the image of its war-torn self. 'Despite appearances, every element of the park is structurally sound' had been the message stressed repeatedly during the promo we'd watched prior to booking. This was a battleground sanctioned by health and safety.

Serna became the first, the biggest, the most famous Warzone Theme Park, and a previously obscure term entered common parlance: Wourism.

Our route from the projection room took us through a corridor lined with display cases housing various small items. I stopped before one: a child's soft toy, a grimy orange-brown teddy bear, with the left eye missing and the left side of its face sooty and blackened.

Sensing my presence, an audio commentary started up, explaining that the bear had been pulled from the rubble of a flattened building during the clean up. Nobody knew the name of its owner or if they'd survived, though several bodies were also recovered at the scene.

I became conscious of somebody standing beside me and looked round to see the woman in the burgundy suit. Close-up, she looked younger than I'd first thought, though her face had that lived-in quality which makes age such a difficult thing to judge.

We smiled at one another and she said, "I used to have a bear just like that, before the war."

"Were you…?" I didn't like to ask.

"I was in Serna during the siege, yes. I was eleven when it started."

I had no idea what to say, rejecting several possibilities which struck me as little more than platitudes; the sort of thing that I would cringe about later.

Fortunately, Alex came back just then. "Come on, Ginny, keep up, it's the big guns next." So he had noticed my absence after all. I nodded to the woman and went with him.

The 'big guns' proved to be imposing, grim, and soulless—chunky blocks of metal in grey or green, sheets of armour plating in pristine mottled camouflage paint, long barrels with gaping muzzles, compact but powerful flat-bodied drone tanks, swivelling turrets, field generators, heat-diffusion nets, projection boards, pulse guns, multiple missile launchers, a stack of lethally indiscriminate pepper mines, some 'smart' bombs, a cluster of artillery shells standing on end and arranged aesthetically in order of size so that their tips created a graceful curve, even a pair of gleaming white snub-winged UAVs—which the hovering 3D sign haughtily designated 'Unmanned Aerial Vehicles'.

Alex got to sit in the control seat of one array, which gyrated in a series of rapid swivels and tilts under his inexpert control.

Gretchen tried to be sociable while Alex fooled around but I wasn't in the mood. Despite having been genuinely moved by Jasna Petrović's account I was beginning to have serious misgivings about this trip. Alex and I had been together for six months now and this was our first time away as a 'couple'. He'd been pressing me to move in with him in recent weeks. At that particular moment, I couldn't have been more delighted that I'd demurred.

It wasn't just Alex, though; it was Serna and all that the place represented.

The entire venture was a delicate balancing act. Initially, revenue from the park had helped to stimulate the local economy and contributed significantly to the city's recovery. Latterly, that economy had come to rely on the flow of income and jobs provided by the park. That was how I'd justified coming along in the first place: this wasn't exploitation at all but something that actually *benefited* the local community. So, now that I was here, why did I feel vaguely... grubby? Why did this whole setup strike me as little more than morbid voyeurism?

"I might head back to the hotel for a long soak in the bath and a lie down..." I said to Alex as we left the big guns behind.

"What? Why?"

"Just feeling a bit tired."

"Oh, come on, Ginny, you can't desert me. You know I won't enjoy myself if you're not here." *Liar!* "Besides, we've spent a lot of money to experience this park," he meant that he had, "so let's experience it! Plenty of time to lie down later... I'll give you a back rub." The accompanying leer offered a more honest indication of what he really hoped to give me.

I should have left at that point despite his objections but knew that he would be shirty and insufferable all evening if I did, so I stayed. To keep the peace; which held a certain irony given the setting.

It was warm outside but not oppressively so. Our party piled onto the minibus—a lozenge-shaped vehicle, its sides more glass than metal. I ended up sitting next to Hassan, with Alex beside Gretchen's explosion of blonde curls in the seat directly in front of us.

There was no driver; the bus was electric and automatic, straddling a guide rail. Malcolm perched by the windscreen and ran through his slick patter as we moved along damaged but eerily silent streets—empty apart from an identical bus a fixed distance ahead of us and another a similar distance behind. I listened with half an ear as Malcolm pointed out the school which famed songstress Andjela had attended as a child—now a ruin—and the church that had been struck by a shell in the midst of a packed service. The entire congregation survived without injury as the shell embedded itself in the pulpit and miraculously failed to detonate.

The bus became a sea of raised hands and perminals as people recorded the various sites for posterity, swaying in unison like wheat in the wind as Malcolm directed our attention from one side of the road to the other. Except for Alex, who had his head bowed and was doubtless using his own perminal to check the football scores.

Many of the buildings we passed were burned out or had their walls marred by strafing lines of bullet holes, recurring pockmarks forever chewed into their substance, while the roadway was frequently pitted by potholes and shell craters—it was often difficult to distinguish which was which—and I couldn't help but wonder whether any restoration work had been carried out at all in some places. There was no attempt to let us out for a closer look.

Not for the first time I found myself wondering what the hell I was doing here. On this tour. In this relationship.

When the bus eventually stopped and we exited, I noticed that Gretchen was flirting with Alex. I also noticed that I didn't care.

Thankfully, the authentic recreation of Serna Under Siege didn't extend to lunch, which we were free to enjoy in a vast courtyard surrounded by an assortment of overpriced fast food outlets and souvenir shops. The place was packed. While we were on the bus the cloud cover had broken and it was now noticeably warmer. Alex went to find us something to drink and a marginally overweight man with red cheeks and sweaty forehead attempted to chat me up. I don't think Alex even noticed. He came back with a couple of fruit-flavoured waters—more ice than anything else—which we greedily sucked up through candy-striped plastic straws.

Gretchen and Hassan were queuing for something and Alex had disappeared in search of the gents when I spotted the woman in the burgundy suit again. On impulse I went across to her and said, in a classic example of transference, "Excuse me, I hope you don't mind me asking, but why are you here?"

Her smile reassured me that she didn't mind in the least. "To remember," she said. "Time has a way of anaesthetising things, of papering over wounds so that memories lose their edge, and I never want to forget what it was like during the siege, what we went through... the horrors that man is capable of inflicting on his fellows."

Her answer stayed with me. On the surface you'd think she had the least reason of any of us to be here, but it turned out she was the only one with a reason that made real sense at all.

After lunch we regrouped and were ushered into an air-conditioned theatre, far larger than the projection room where we'd encountered the shade of Jasna Petrović. Ours was just one of several parties that were herded in here. I made a point of ensuring we sat next to the woman in the burgundy suit, telling myself that she was here on her own and would be glad of a familiar face. In fact, I suspect I took more strength from her presence than she did from mine.

For the best part of an hour we were treated to an illustrated talk by a Professor Something-or-Other, an eminent social historian retained by the theme park. He was animated, his descriptions vivid and the many images he employed graphic, but I could tell that Alex was getting restless. He didn't want to hear about the grim realities of surviving the siege, of squalid conditions and dysentery and the bravery of hard-pressed civilians. He wouldn't admit as much but the only reason he'd come here was for guns and explosions. To Alex, Serna was the ultimate wargame: he got to play where it *really* happened.

Not so long ago, his boyish enthusiasm matched with bullish self-confidence had seemed to me endearing, attractive. Now, I could only wonder why.

The following day was scheduled to be the centrepiece of the trip: the principal reason Alex had been so eager to come to Serna. We were to discover what it had been like to live here during the war, by taking part in a re-enactment. We would form our own unit of the local militia and fight a guerrilla action amongst the broken buildings and the rubble, defending the city against a heavily armed force of invading troops. I had already decided that Alex would enter the fray without me. That evening I intended to pack my bags and head for home.

The finale of the professor's talk involved a frail and elderly man being helped onto the stage. He was introduced as a survivor of the Siege of Serna. We all clapped.

As the applause died away, Alex leaned over and murmured, "Yes, but it was all so long ago. What the hell does any of this really matter to anyone now?"

I glanced across at the woman in the burgundy suit. I'm sure that Alex had meant his words for my ears alone, but he'd spoken more loudly than necessary and the woman had clearly heard him.

Our eyes met. For an unguarded instant I saw the hurt there. She recovered quickly, even managing to smile, and at that moment it seemed that we two were the only real people in the room.

Montpellier

Montpellier is a shithole. I didn't want to go there in the first place but nor did anyone else and I was too slow in coming up with an excuse.

There are four of them: Montpellier, Biscay, Siena, and Detroit. Officially termed 'habitat complexes', they are known locally as the Four Horsemen. War hasn't actually broken out there yet, but three out of four ain't bad. Besides, give it time...

The Horsemen form an off-kilter diamond in an unfashionable downtown suburb of Victoria—the part of the city the tourists never see. Uptown the theme is eco-balance and elegance—leafy avenues lined with glitzy store fronts, pocket parks and hidden arboreta with tinkling water features and shaded paths and flower beds—all designed to relax the weary shopper after a morning's indulgence. Downtown, not so much. Anything growing has been eaten, smoked, or chopped down for winter fuel long ago.

I took the subway, not wanting to risk my own vehicle anywhere near the place. A state of the art security system doesn't s discourage the resourceful thief, it merely inspires them. I should know. You see, my mistrust of the Horsemen isn't born of cultural prejudice or media-fed ignorance, quite the opposite. I was born here. In Montpellier. That's why when this job was passed to me it stuck, having already been shifted hastily along by a number of wiser colleagues. The assumption being that my heritage would give me some sort of advantage. Like hell. Anyone born in the Horsemen spends their waking hours dreaming of getting out and automatically despises those who've managed to.

As I exited the subway it was raining. A monotonous drizzle, not heavy but relentless, as if determined to pummel the world into submission by a process of attrition. Around me were small houses with leaky roofs and water pooling in their doorways. Dark scowls followed me along the road—nosy old women peering out from windows, round-shouldered punks sheltering in porches. I didn't fit. My clothes marked me as an outsider. Oh, I'd tried to dress down, but these days even my tattiest gear made me look like an uptown fuckwit that had got off at the wrong stop.

If the Horsemen form a diamond it's a rough one, knobbly and uncut. The components are towering edifices that thrust up from low-rise streets like broken teeth dislodged from the jawbone of some long-dead leviathan. Around and between them the squalor has leaked outward, uniting the district in poverty and grime. Or that's how it's always seemed to me. Truth is that this was a run-down neighbourhood before the Horsemen were constructed, while they were being constructed, and ever since they came to dominate the skyline. That's just how it is. Self-contained communities with spacious apartments, schools, parks, shops, health centres, everything necessary to ensure a decent standard of living, the habitats were supposed to change all that. Not that anyone local ever bought into the hype. Sure enough, the money ran out. The promised support dried up. Immediately after the official opening—pats on the back and self-congratulatory handshakes all round despite the project being delivered nearly a year late—the authorities forgot about downtown, turning their attention elsewhere. Others moved in to fill the void.

Ill-conceived and chronically under-funded, the new communities floundered before they'd properly begun. Downtown won. Instead of lifting the whole district out of the relentless mire of poverty as idealists had predicted, the habitats were dragged down into it. The Horsemen were born. They became the symbol of everything squalid and distasteful about downtown, both in public perception and in reality.

Any wonder I didn't relish coming back here?

Ahead of me rose the jagged outline of the Horsemen, with Montpellier the closest at the southern tip of the diamond. At odd moments the sun struggled to break through; a watery orb drooping low and miserable over the city as if even it had fallen victim to the general malaise and lacked the energy to climb higher. Presumably there was a rainbow somewhere, but not here. I trudged forward, hands in pockets, staring at the puddles, avoiding eye contact. I wasn't really expecting trouble, at least nothing I couldn't handle, but out here at the periphery you never could tell. The punks hanging around at this point were outliers—petty dealers and hotheads at the bottom of the pecking order—minnows. Even the minnows had teeth, though, and there was no guarantee that one of them, anxious to build a rep or simply bored, mightn't fancy shaking down a stranger just for the hell of it. So I kept my head bowed, having neither the time nor the patience to spare.

I was fully expecting to be challenged on reaching Montpellier itself, but that was fine. My employers benefited from off-world backing. The petty gang lords who squabbled over the Horsemen's avenues and corridors weren't about to risk messing with that sort of muscle. And if an ambitious lieutenant took it into their head to take me on, more fool them. Not so long ago I had been where they were now, except that I was better, which is how I got out.

Funny thing about being a lookout: you have to make it seem you're loitering without actually loitering at all. I spotted the first three as I came up to the entrance—not the *main* entrance, Montpellier doesn't have a *main* entrance. The plaque identifying this one had been defaced, but I didn't need it. This was SE3-Red, the 'Red' indicating which quadrant of the habitat the entrance led into, so why they bothered with the 'South East' bit is anyone's guess. I had a total of nine customers to call on and four of them lived in Red, so it seemed as good a place as any to start. Personal visits weren't exactly the norm, but nine customers defaulting within the same week made for exceptional circumstances.

Finding three kids by the entrance didn't come as a surprise. Their avatars did.

A crouching scorpion flickered in and out of view around the lanky, skinny lad—tail raised to match his height, sting to the fore—that one was familiar. The Scorpions had been a major presence in Red since my time. The other two—a vortex of swirling wind that circled the swarthy girl and the menacing black-furred ape sported by the twitchy, stocky boy—were new to me. Gangs came and went in the Horsemen with such rapidity it was hard to keep track. The fun part when you don't recognise gang affiliations is to allocate your own. Doubtless these two belonged to something relating to tornadoes and gorillas respectively, but I chose to think of them as Windy and Baboon.

The surprise lay in the variety. Entrances were coveted as income generators. Security normally represented the gang in possession, and this had always been Scorpion territory. It wasn't unheard of for gang members to intermingle socially, but at a gate?

The girl took the lead, stepping out from the overhang she'd been sheltering under to confront me. The other two backed her up—Scorpion to the left, Baboon on the right.

"You lost?" Rain dripped off the peak of her sodden cap. She didn't look especially menacing despite her best attempt.

"No," I assured her. "Official business." I activated my own avatar. I didn't sport mine all the time—such things aren't appropriate to the circles I tend to move in—but it was there when needed. Unlike theirs, mine was a seamless projection. It didn't flicker on and off so that one moment you were staring at a stylized emblem, the next the person behind it. In my stead the kids would now be facing a solid-seeming white-cowled figure, face invisible within a deep hood, both hands gripping the pommel of a broadsword with its tip resting on the ground.

"Saflik!" the girl hissed. It means 'purity'. My employers were idealists and the name held significance for them that was lost on me. Its impact wasn't. All three kids tensed, and I could swear the baboon actually shuffled backwards a step.

I killed the avatar and smiled.

It took a moment but the girl stepped aside. I didn't doubt that somebody had instructed her to do so, whispering in her ear. Without another word I walked forward. Two to my left, one to my right, all three of them looked relieved to see me pass.

There were no actual doors, just an archway. The Horsemen were never meant to be sealed communities, merely self-sufficient—the planners had no intention of either locking the world out or the inhabitants in.

Now that I was here I dropped the act. No more skulking, no more deference. I belonged here. I *owned* this place. A man called Baxter was supposed to run the Scorpions these days— after my time and I hadn't met him. He would already be aware of my presence. Maybe others were too. Still couldn't get my head around the mixed nature of the reception committee. Things in Montpellier were clearly changing.

A door slammed somewhere over to my left as I walked through the archway and into the open courtyard beyond. There was nobody in sight, nobody at all. The weather seemed wilder here, perhaps funnelled by the solid block of building that surrounded the exposed courtyard. Whipped by the wind, rain beat against the paving and the cobbles in a muffled tattoo, barely louder than a sigh but never letting up: nature's drumroll heralding my arrival. I heard the laughter and shriek of young children at play from high above—the sound made flat and oddly muted by the rain—and a woman shouting at them to shut up, but these were isolated noises. Otherwise, there was just the rain. It was bizarre. This was a community, where was everybody? Had they fled, warned of my approach?

Maybe they were simply staying inside to keep dry.

I took the walkway on my right, impressed that the thing was still working—it hadn't always been when I was a kid. There were no stairs or elevators in the Horsemen, just long sweeping paths and travelators like this, which carried the populace up or down at a gentle incline. Accessibility was king.

The mural that adorned the wall beside me had been hijacked years ago. Originally it depicted an idealised pastoral scene in 3D relief—cornfields swaying in a gentle breeze, a stand of trees, birds flitting around a hedgerow—with the light changing throughout the day to reflect the hour and prevailing weather conditions. Doubtless meant to lighten our spirits, it had been completely irrelevant to everyone here. Currently my trip upwards was accompanied by a scene of bumbling erotica in painstaking close-up. Not sure if this was intended to be comical, but that's how it came across. Giant buttocks heaving as I passed. In an hour or so there would be something different, depending on the hackers' whim.

I stepped off at the third level, which provoked an unexpected wave of nostalgia—I'd grown up not far from here. Ahead, in a sheltered corridor, a man sat on an old wooden chair. The first person I'd seen since entering Montpellier. He was leaning forward, working on something. This too stimulated a welter of memories. I knew this man: Case. Sitting outside his home watching the world go by, just as he always had. As I drew closer I could see that he was whittling away at a piece of pale wood with a penknife. Too early to say what he was carving.

He'd changed. His face had wrinkled into a cartographer's dream, a canvas of deep crevices and mysterious contours. Still alert though, still savvy. Still Case. He looked up as I approached, sharp eyes peering like obsidian coals from his weathered visage. "Horner," he said, his voice as strong as ever. "Welcome home."

The way he spoke you'd think I had just popped out for some groceries rather than been gone for the best part of a decade.

"Case," I acknowledged. "How's things?"

Case had been a big noise back in the day. Not gang affiliated, not beholden to any of the petty lords who came and went more frequently than a cat takes a piss, but somehow respected by all of them. Case didn't need to move around much, the world came to him. He had women too. One in particular always used to give the adolescent me a hard on. Lizzie her name was. Not exactly a classic beauty but you knew she'd be worth the effort—dyed blonde hair, big boobs that seemed on the verge of bursting out from her tight leather jacket, and a smile that made you think you stood a chance even when deep down you knew that was bullshit. I wondered if Lizzie was still around, whether she was still with Case, and I pictured how she'd look now, her teeth yellowed from smokes and her big tits saggy and pendulous or shrivelled and wrinkled like prunes. One of her knowing smiles would probably still get my juices going, though.

"Same old same old," Case said. "You got business here?"

"Yes."

"Saflik business?"

How well connected *was* he, anyway? "Yes."

"Good luck with that."

He went back to his whittling. I walked on, wondering what that had been about. Sure as hell the encounter hadn't happened by chance. Word must have reached him straight from the gate, and Case wanted to let me know that he knew why I was here, but to what purpose? To warn me, to warn me *off*, or simply to prepare me for something? And who did Case represent? One thing was certain: there was far more going on at Montpellier than anyone back at Saflik realised.

I rounded a corner and a snarling demon leapt off the wall to attack me. I ignored it and kept walking. The graffiti was getting more sophisticated—this one had found a way around my blocks. It brought a small sense of pride. Good to know that ingenuity like this was still alive and kicking in Montpellier.

First call on my list was one Eleanor 'Ellie' Drew, 73 Scarlet Walk. To get there I'd have to go out into the open again. Rain obscured the view across to the opposite buttress of apartments— part of Blue quadrant. The sun had now disappeared altogether, presumably writing the day off and determining to save its energy for tomorrow. Good move.

I scrolled through Eleanor's details, scant though they were: twenty-six years old, two kids—three and five—fathers unknown; busted three times for prostitution, the most recent two years ago; no apparent means of financial support, no apparent reason to love reality. In short, ideal customer material.

My employers had their fingers in many pies. One of the most lucrative was narcotics, e-drugs: no pills swallowed, no needles required. Chemical narcotics were as passé as dinosaurs. Every aspect of a deal now took place online, with e-hits sold in batches; data-squirts that, when triggered, delivered stimulation directly to specifically targeted areas of the brain. Swift, clean, no-nonsense transactions. The lowlifes in the Horsemen got the crude, straightforward shit, far less refined than the hits pedalled to lawyers and politicians, to business women and bureaucrats who formed our client base uptown—many of those hits were personalised, tailored to an individual's genetic signature—but whatever the grade, the result was still as addictive as anything a chemist might cook up. And that was the clincher.

To lose one client could be chalked up as bad luck—people died, got thrown in jail, or found the inspiration to try to kick the habit—but *nine* in the same place at the same time went way beyond coincidence. It meant something else. Competition. Somebody was muscling in on Saflik business.

I knocked.

She was tall, thin to the point of being gaunt, eyes as blank as her prospects, resigned to whatever crap life threw at her.

"Ellie Drew? My name's Horner. I'm from Saflik."

"Yeah, I've been expecting you."

Evidently. She wasn't alone, as I discovered when she took me through to the sitting room. A man lounged on the sofa. She didn't introduce him, may not even have known his name. Black, built like a compact car. His left arm rested along the back of the settee, stretching from one end to the other. The can of beer he clutched in his right hand was dwarfed by his fist. A mean-looking bastard, for all that he was trying to appear relaxed.

The image of a scorpion flickered on and off around him.

Her two kids were nowhere in sight.

The decks had been cleared in anticipation of a fight.

No point in delaying. I already knew how this was going to pan out, but I had my part to play. "We've been worried about you, Ellie," I said. "You haven't renewed and we're concerned that something may have…"

"She don't need any more o' your shit," the big man said without looking at me. He was staring straight ahead, as if absorbed in VR, but he wasn't wearing a visor and I couldn't detect any lenses.

"If it's been a tough month and you can't meet the payment," I said, ignoring him and addressing her, "that's not a problem, we can work something out."

"It ain't," Big Man said. "She just don't want what you're sellin'." He still refused to look at me.

Could I take him? Probably, but it wouldn't be quick or easy.

I glanced at Ellie and saw the first hint of animation in her eyes: desperation. She didn't want to see her place trashed. She was scared of me, maybe of him, and certainly of what we were likely to do between us.

I took pity. I didn't doubt now that all nine of my errant customers would have chaperones and I didn't doubt that there was a fight brewing somewhere down the line, but it didn't have to be here. Ellie was no different from my mom, rest her soul, or from thousands of others like her throughout the Horsemen. Just trying to get by. She didn't need this.

"Think about what I said, Ellie. I'll call back later."

As I left the big man said something. I didn't catch the words but I didn't need to. The tone said more than enough: something scornful, something derogatory, something about me being a coward. That almost did it, almost had me tossing all my good intentions aside and turning around to smash his smug face in... But I kept walking.

Outside, six doors down, were two kids: a Scorpion and a Wildcat—another of the long-established gangs dating back to my day. Remember what I said about loitering? They were doing that.

I was about to turn right, towards the next address on my list, but changed my mind. Instead I headed left, towards them. If there was going to be a confrontation, might as well be out here in the open rather than in someone's home. The space was narrow if it came to a fight, with a sheer drop on one side and a brick wall on the other, but what the hell?

The Scorp was a scrawny girl, the Cat a tall lad who hadn't quite grown into his frame yet but still looked the greater threat. I bore down on them before they could do much more than stop loitering.

"Take me to see Baxter or whoever the fuck is running things nowadays," I said.

The Cat attempted a sneer. It looked comical. "Why would Baxter want...?"

I hit him. He went down in a heap, out for the count with one punch. I figured with him out the way the girl would be easy. My mistake. She kicked me. Nothing behind it—she was too slight to do real damage—but well-directed and delivered like a pro: swivel, kick, spin away, bouncing on her toes, ready for the next strike. I feinted towards her and she was at it again, a roundhouse kick that caught me on the hip before she danced back out of reach. That one hurt. Shit! I knew what this was: Kix—a hybrid martial art that had evolved in downtown, marrying together elements from various classic disciplines—and she knew her stuff.

I got lucky, though. As I feinted again and she kicked again I guessed right and caught her foot, fastening on to her ankle and refusing to let go. Like I said, there was nothing of her. Before she could twist free I had both hands locked on, swinging her around to slam against the wall. She struck the brickwork hard but that didn't stop her cursing and bucking and kicking out at me with the other foot. I tugged and heaved and swung her into the wall again. The second time did the trick.

The fight had mostly gone out of her as I dragged her upright, holding her by the throat. "Now, where can I find Baxter?"

"Right here." It was a woman's voice, coming from behind me.

I turned to see a dozen or more punks crowding the terrace. And they all looked eager for a piece of me. Scorpions, Wildcats, Dragons, Pirates, Baboons and more I didn't recognise flickered in and out like spectres at a feast.

As one, the front rank parted and a woman strode through. Hourglass figure, well-built and with a mass of blonde hair. Older than any of the others... and I knew her.

"Lizzie?" No sagging tits, no yellowed teeth or pasty jowls. In fact, she looked fantastic.

"You can call me Baxter," and she grinned, clearly enjoying my surprise. "What, Horny Boy," the name she'd always teased me with, "you expected someone with balls? Now put Asa down, will you? We need to talk."

With that she turned and walked away, the gang members shuffling aside as if she was some kind of royalty. I dropped Kicking Girl and followed.

She led the way to an apartment, no different to any of the others, except that a Scorpion and a Lion stood sentry by the door.

"Beer?" she asked once we were inside.

Nobody else had come in, the motley escort that had followed us here stopping short at the threshold.

"Sure."

The place was as ordinary as it had seemed on the outside. Nothing gaudy, nothing flash, nothing to suggest that here lived the ruling power in Montpellier. We sat on a sofa, angled towards each other, knees almost touching. Two old friends catching up. There was no hint of tension in her posture, no suggestion that she was anything other than relaxed and in control. Wish I could have said the same.

Here was the woman I'd fantasised about as a kid, looking hotter than ever, and I was alone with her. At the same time, here was the person I had to deal with, make demands of and ensure she toed the line. I didn't know where to start. Fortunately, she did.

"I want your help, Horny Boy," she said. "I'm doing things here, important things, but it takes time, and I need the space to operate without Saflik interfering. These e-drugs your employers are pushing, they're screwing things up big time. They're designed to be addictive, stimulating the brain to produce a surge of dopamine and controlling its interaction with other neurotransmitters like glutamate. You know about dopamine? Impressive stuff, *powerful* stuff. It not only induces a sense of pleasure, of euphoria, but lays down the memory of that pleasure, in effect rewiring the brain to crave it again and again.

"Saflik have hit on a goldmine. The only real outlay for these e-hits lies in the initial development and programming. Once you have that, you can produce and distribute to your heart's content at the push of a button, which is why Saflik can afford to flood the market with cheap, low grade narc. It's money for nothing. But what is the market here at the Horsemen *really* worth to them compared to what they get from the movers and shakers uptown?"

Not much, but that wasn't the point. Saflik wouldn't view things that way. No matter how trivial the market it was *their* market, and they couldn't afford to be seen as weak.

"You know what life's like here," Lizzie continued. "Is it any wonder that our people seize on an affordable escape when it's offered? By preying on their weakness Saflik are *destroying* this place! How can we make progress when everyone with a scrap of drive and imagination gets hooked on their shit? So I'm doing something about it."

"You've united the gangs," I said. A bland statement that didn't come close to conveying how impressed I was. I would have sworn blind that gang unity was impossible, the enmity and petty rivalries too deeply rooted. Yet, somehow, Lizzie had achieved it.

"Eventually," she said. "You've no idea how hard that was or how long it took. With Case's help I've been working on this since before you left Montpellier. But that's only the beginning. Now we want to move on, to really build something, to let the habitats shake off the shackles of being 'The Four Horsemen' and become what they were always meant to be. A place where people can thrive, not merely survive.

"So our programmers have come up with a way to counter your e-drugs, to dampen the release of dopamine and rewire the brain so that it no longer recalls the hit as unbearably pleasurable but merely pleasant. Doesn't mean that people can't enjoy a high now and again, just that they don't crave it."

I stared at her. I'd never heard of anything like this before. "Seriously?"

"Yeah. I told you, we mean business."

Clearly.

"All we need is someone to persuade Saflik to back off."

I didn't like the way this was going, not one bit. "Now wait a minute…"

"We've got a chance here, Horny Boy" she pressed, "an opportunity to really make something of this place at last. You're one of the lucky ones, you got out, but what about all the people who haven't and who never will?"

God only knew what she had me down as. "You're overestimating my importance," I told her.

"I don't think so. Saflik sent you here to report on what's going on. By definition they're gonna listen to what you have to say. That gives you power."

"For fuck sake, Lizzie. You don't know these people. Saflik aren't interested in making a better future for Montpellier or for anyone else. To them it's all about access to market and profit, and you're blocking the way to both. However I try to paint things they're just gonna see you as a threat." Not even a threat, more an inconvenience. "They'll *have* to make an example of you. Unless…"

"What?"

"Unless you can persuade them it's worth their while not to, unless you can offer them something in return, something more valuable than you're asking them to give up." The higher ups at Saflik couldn't muster an altruistic bone between them, but they were capable of seeing the bigger picture.

"Go on."

I was thinking on my feet, but as I spoke I knew that this was right, that it offered a chance, the *only* chance for Lizzie and her vision of a brighter future for Montpellier and its people; *my* people. "The programmers and splicers, the hackers and freesurfers: the kids who came up with countermeasures to the e-drugs, the ones who hijack the murals and can design graffiti that sneaks past the strongest firewalls… That's what you offer them."

"I dunno…"

"Think about it. This wouldn't be a betrayal. You said it yourself, I got out. They can too, in a way that'll benefit everyone. They can continue doing stuff for you, for the community, but also be on Saflik's payroll." Saflik would fall over backwards for talent like this. It was worth writing off a few low-grade drug contracts for, and they could do so without losing face because they would be gaining a resource in exchange.

"Will they go for that?"

"I'll make sure they do, pitch it to them in a way they can't refuse, tell them it's the only way your people will work for them. You've got skills here; *that's* your leverage. Use it. You can act as Saflik's agent, a recruiter. The Horsemen will become a kind of feeder project for grassroot talent, starting with Montpellier, and that'll buy you the time to complete what you've begun, the authority to push it through. Hell, Saflik might even pump some of their own money into what you're doing for that sort of opportunity." I paused. "There's just one thing."

"What?"

"If I do this, I'm taking one hell of a risk. There's always a chance Saflik could reject the whole idea and stop trusting me as a result, accuse me of going native. I could lose everything... So what's in it for me?"

"You want a cut...?"

"Not exactly." I reached out and touched her knee.

She laughed, a deep, sultry sound. "Really, Horny Boy? Still? Even though I'm an old woman now?"

"Not so old, and... Yeah."

She leant forward to plant a kiss on my cheek, and at the same time removed my hand from her knee. "That's very flattering, but let's just see how this all pans out and take it from there, shall we?"

So I left without even copping a feel, but I brought with me the memory of her lips on my cheek and I had hope, which is as much as I'd ever had where Lizzie was concerned.

I also had hope for Montpellier, which was *more* than I'd ever had before.

No Smoke Without Fire

I have to admit, there was a time when I feared for the traditional London pub. So many favourite watering holes had disappeared, to be lamented with a raised glass and sorrowful shake of the head. The spread of the wine bar had faltered, true, but the baton had been taken up by the tapas bar and the brand-name chains. Dark beams, uneven floors, tables whose legs were never quite stable no matter what combination of folded drinks mats you slipped beneath their feet and whose surfaces had been seasoned by generations of beer stains, cigarette ash and tall tales, all swept away as if they had never been. One day a familiar, much-loved boozer, the next a restricted zone, guarded by the dreaded sign, 'Closed for Renovation'.

We all knew what that meant: transformation; high ceilings, bright open spaces, rows of light-wood tables with identical matching chairs, gleaming chrome swan-necked beer pumps serving continental lagers with suspicious names, each new re-opening indistinguishable from the last, the whole staffed by fresh-faced trendies in starch-white shirts and blouses. Another character-infused London landmark sacrificed on the altar of homogeneity.

Of course, I need not have worried. Like wine bars before them, the poured-from-a-mould pubs made inroads but then faltered, as if hitting some impassable line drawn in the sand with arcane purpose: 'Thou Shalt Come No Further!' The London pub survives, as it always has, and, I suspect, as it always will.

In truth, my *real* concern in the matter focused on just one pub in particular; the Fountain. No, not the *Old* Fountain in Baldwin Street, close to Old Street Station, redoubtable establishment though that may be. Ours is simply *the* Fountain, and it's timeless.

At first glance the Fountain is not perhaps the most spectacular of buildings. It is homely, welcoming, with a hint of mock Tudor in its bold facade... and somehow *right*. Nor is it the easiest place to find, I'll grant you, and all the better for that. The Fountain is in Holborn, within a short walk of Chancery Lane tube and Lincoln's Inn Fields. It nestles on one of the network of little lanes that leads eventually to the far broader Chancery Lane, though I've never yet managed to arrive there by the same route twice. It's the sort of hidden gem you come upon unexpectedly when cutting down towards the Strand and Fleet Street without any clear idea of the way. You might stumble upon the Fountain and slow down, perhaps make a mental note to come back here sometime, only to never find the place again. You see, there's little point in my explaining *how* to get there; either you will, or you won't.

There are, of course, several reasons why we meet at the Fountain rather than any of the City's other hostelries. It's the perfect size, for one. On a good night, we can all but fill out the back room, the Paradise bar—which is really just a partitioned extension of the lounge with its own small door to the outside world. I say 'we', but that small word encompasses a flexible roster of dynamic components. There are regulars such as Brian Dalton, who is a chemist, Professor Mackintosh—our geo-metrodynamics theoretician—Dr Steve, whose voice I'd heard even before we met, since he frequently guests on radio programmes offering listeners advice on back pain and other ailments, and Ray Arnold, a man around whom it's never advisable to quip 'it's not rocket science', since where Ray's concerned it often is. He worked for the European Space Agency in the Netherlands before returning to these shores a while back.

There are also the irregulars, such as Eric, a Yorkshireman living in exile in Cambridgeshire, a professional author who can't join us every week due to family commitments, though he travels in whenever he can; and then there's the Raven. A somewhat dramatic moniker, admittedly, but that's what we took to calling the dark brooding presence with his long hair, beard, and painful-looking piercings, before we actually met him. Every now and then he'd be there on a Tuesday—our night—always at the same table in the corner, alone; sitting at the fringes, listening, watching; an enigmatic, swashbuckling figure. Until we came to know him a little better that is, and discovered that he goes by the decidedly mundane name of Paul and is a librarian.

Tuesday; I'm not quite sure *why* we settled on that night in particular, except that Tuesdays aren't Fridays, when *everyone* descends on the nearest pub after work, and nor are they Thursdays, when those seeking to avoid Fridays tend to do the same. So Tuesdays it is.

When I refer to the Fountain as a 'traditional' London pub, I don't mean to imply that it's a complete anachronism, far from it. Michael, the landlord, is quite happy to see the place move with the times, he's merely selective about *which* times he moves with. So while bottles of Mexican beer lurk in the chill cabinet and you might on occasion be served by Eastern European bar staff—Bogna from Poland was particularly popular, as I recall— no jukebox or fruit machine stands sentry by the wall, and no plasma screen TV churns out live coverage of the latest big game; not at the Fountain. Such things would be out of place among the beams and framed pictures of Victorian London that adorn ceiling and walls respectively. I've a mind to suggest they might even sour the fine selection of ales that are invariably on offer at the many hand pumps. One recent concession to progress that Michael *has* made is to affix a bench to the outside wall of the pub, where a narrow passageway runs between one lane and another. This for the convenience of smokers—there's no 'beer garden' of course, not in central London where space is at such a premium.

I confess to viewing the smoking ban as a sort of guilty pleasure. I'm not a smoker, never have been, but when the ban was first mooted I felt far from comfortable with the idea of central government dictating to the individual in such a way, and by the time the reality of the legislation loomed large, I found myself objecting strongly. Yet, now that the ban is actually here, I'm secretly delighted that it is—pubs and restaurants are so much more pleasant for those of us who don't partake of the old baccy. Hence the guilt.

Others were less ambiguous in their objection. Take Professor Mackintosh, for example. When the ban was first enforced he took to sporting a pipe, either chewing on its stem or holding it by the bowl and gesturing dramatically when making a point. Oh, don't get me wrong, the pipe was neither lit nor indeed filled and I can't recall him toting such a thing with any regularity prior to the ban. No, I believe this was simply the Professor's way of making silent protest.

I remember one particular Tuesday. There was a good crowd in that evening; I was sharing a table with Crown Baker and Eric—both science fiction writers so always entertaining—while Professor Mackintosh was beside me, at the next table.

"Smoking once saved my life, you know," he declared as he reached across to tap his pipe against the side of the hearth, as if to free non-existent embers from the bowl.

"Really?" I felt obliged to ask.

"Oh, yes."

Such a pronouncement did not go unnoticed, needless to say, and within moments a group had gathered around us, the professor waiting patiently while feet shuffled and chairs scraped, as people manoeuvred into hearing range.

"All down to an acquaintance of mine, Edward Blaycock," he then continued. "Interesting fellow, old Blaycock. He had a passion for collecting religious books; not merely those *about* religion, either. As well as various rare editions of the bible, the Koran, the Tao Te Ching etcetera, he had a truly impressive collection of prayer books, hymn books and missals…"

"Missals?" I asked.

"Yes, liturgical volumes containing the texts and formulae for use in various church services."

"So I suppose a scathing attack on the content of a church service would be a *dis*-missal?"

There were a few appreciative groans from the assembled throng, while the prof stared at me blankly for a second, as if I'd spoken in an unfamiliar language, and then chuckled. "Ah yes, very good." Though his tone implied the contrary.

"By day," he went on, "Blaycock was a scientist. He worked

at the Yarlsbury Research Centre in Lincolnshire, not far from Market Rasen, usually on matters that were extremely hush-hush. I was there for a year or so in an advisory capacity and worked with Blaycock on a project relating to Electromagnetic Pulse weaponry. We were tasked with developing a defence against the triple component EMP effect of a high-altitude nuclear explosion. This meant designing countermeasures to all three stages—the three are designated in accordance with the speed of their respective effects. E2, the middle one, isn't such a threat on its own. Its impact is similar to that of a localised lightning strike and can be countered with standard measures... unless those standard defences have already been knocked out by the higher amplitude E1. This is the fastest of the three components—a field generated when gamma rays from the explosion collide with electrons in the air molecules of the upper atmosphere. These electrons are punched out from their parent molecules at close to the speed of light, colliding with others and causing a cascade effect that's analogous to a sonic boom. The interaction of all these electrons with the Earth's magnetic field produces a very brief but intense electromagnetic pulse; very difficult to defend against. The E3 component causes problems all its own. Much slower than the first two, the impact of E3 is similar to that of a really big solar flare, which can cause havoc with the Earth's magnetosphere—the sort of thing that disrupted power supplies throughout Quebec in 1989.

"So E1 and E3 were our real targets, and buggers to deal with they were too. Brilliant chap, though, Blaycock, and he'd already come up with a way of dampening the processes involved in E1. I can't go into details, obviously—national security and all that—but our only real problem was finding a way to trigger the countermeasure quickly enough."

I wasn't sure whether to curse 'national security' or feel relieved; at least this meant avoiding a complicated and doubtless lengthy aside, and I'd already had my fill of E1s and E2s thank you very much.

"Anyway," the professor continued, "those of us involved were summoned to a demonstration one Sunday. Very unusual.

Blaycock was clearly excited about something, and we assumed he'd solved the triggering issue. We were the only people at the centre apart from the security guards on the gate. First thing we did was divest ourselves of anything electrical—laptops, phones, watches—no point in risking them in range of anything relating to EMP—and then we went into 'the bunker'. The bunker is a fair sized room, underground as the name suggests, lead-lined and airtight. The perfect place to test all manner of things."

I could see knowing looks pass amongst my fellow listeners. It would have been rude to interrupt now that the professor was in full flow but you could read people's thoughts clearly enough in those glances: *an experiment goes wrong; something terrible happens.*

"So there we all were, eight of us, sealed away from the rest of the world and anxious to hear Blaycock's big announcement, when it happened.

"Without any warning, the place was hit by...." He paused to cough.

"Lightning," Brian Dalton cut in, politeness evidently forgotten in the heat of the moment.

"A tornado," Eric said.

"A bomb," Crown Baker suggested.

"A terrorist attack," Dr Steve added, as if to give credence to Crown's suggestion.

"A flock of crazed birds," someone else—probably Graham O'Donnell—said, clearly getting carried away.

"No, no, nothing like that," the professor assured us. "It was hit by an earthquake."

"An *earthquake*? In Britain?"

The professor smiled. "Certainly. We suffer around 200 every year believe it or not, though only twenty or so are ever actually felt by anyone."

"And this was one of those," I prompted, concerned that the good prof was about to meander down one of his beloved sidetracks strewn with tangential information.

"Oh yes," he confirmed. "5.8 on the Richter scale—hardly earth-shattering in global terms, if you'll forgive the pun, but certainly significant for the UK. We get hit by a quake at that sort of magnitude just once every thirty years or so.

"As it turned out, the epicentre of this one wasn't far from Yarlsbury, so we felt the full force of it; the whole place shook something terrible. Quite an alarming experience when you're stuck underground in a sealed space, I can tell you. However, as things calmed down we were all greatly relieved to realise that the room remained intact.

"We were just beginning to relax… when the lights went out."

A few murmurs greeted this part of the story and I noticed Crown Baker shudder. Not that I blamed him. The fear of being confined underground in the dark, of being buried alive, is about as primordial and instinctive as it comes.

"Not just the lights were affected, as we soon discovered," the professor continued. "All the power was down, which meant no air conditioning, no external communication system, and—most concerning of all—no means of opening the doors."

"A bit like the effects of an EMP," somebody noted.

"Quite," the prof agreed. "We were well and truly trapped, with no phones or indeed any means of communication, and the only people who even knew we were at the centre were the guards at the gate, who doubtless had their own concerns, what with the facility they were charged to safeguard having just lost its entire security system. Besides, we hadn't told them we were going into the bunker, so there was no reason for them to appreciate the seriousness of our predicament."

"What about back-up generators?" Ray Arnold asked.

"Damaged by the quake," the prof explained, "We were on our own, in the dark, with only a limited amount of air and no immediate prospect of rescue. Realisation began to sink in that somehow, on what had started out as a perfectly unremarkable Sunday, we were facing the very real prospect of dying. You never really know how you're going to react in a situation like that until it actually happens. One or two panicked. It was difficult to tell precisely who was sobbing in the dark, but I could have sworn they included old Blaycock himself. I, on the other hand, kept a remarkably cool head, which was just as well for all concerned."

"So… what did you do?" Eric asked, perhaps realising that the professor wasn't about to continue until *somebody* asked.

"Why, I did what any civilised soul would do… I lit my pipe."

"You did *what*? In a confined room like that?"

"Of course," and the professor grinned. "How else was I going to trigger the smoke alarm?"

"Ah!" Nods and knowing smiles spread throughout the cordon of listeners.

"It was the only thing in the room that possessed its own heavily protected power source and was connected directly to the guard station. I reasoned that security couldn't fail to investigate a potential fire, and, sure enough, they were there within minutes and had us out in no time.

"So don't you go telling *me* that smoking's bad for my health!"

Appreciative chuckles were the prof's principle reward, that and Ray Arnold's offer of another pint. My attention was dragged rudely away from the ensuing discussion courtesy of a strident voice.

"No, no, it's called *the Fountain*."

I turned to scowl at the lad in the wrinkled suit leaning back against the bar; City-type, buttons of his striped shirt undone, no tie in evidence, one ear glued to a sliver of plastic which presumably constituted a phone. His voice was raised to a level suggesting that he didn't entirely trust the flimsy gadget to do the job either.

"It's… ehhm…" He looked around, his gaze meeting mine beseechingly.

"Near Holborn," I supplied, taking pity.

"Yeah, it's near Holborn," he repeated. "Turn right out of Chancery Lane station, take the first right, and then, ehhm… No, no, it's not far. You can't miss it… The Fountain. All right, babe, see you in ten minutes."

I looked at Eric. He looked at me. We shared a smile, and, I feel certain, the same thought: *you'll be lucky.*

For Your Own Good

I stood up and brushed gravel from my bare arms and dust from my trousers. The gravel had left mottled imprints on my skin where I'd been lying on it. I scrambled to my feet and took stock of the surroundings. The sky towards the horizon formed a red wine stain bleeding outwards—spilled claret on linen—and the air had that preternatural stillness which can sometimes precede a storm. It was warm without being oppressive, and I knew instinctively that the day had been a hot one, though cooling rapidly now with the onset of evening. That was about as far as I got before the Big Questions bludgeoned their way to the forefront of thought and left little room for anything else. *Where the hell am I?* being the first to arrive, immediately followed by: *How did I get here?*

I gazed around, uncomprehending. The last thing I remembered was... What exactly?

This was ridiculous. I had a very clear sense of self, of *me*, but couldn't piece together the sequence of events that led to my being here. I should be in the city, immersed in noise and people and grime and environmentally precise air con, not out here in the wilderness under an open sky surrounded by so much stillness and silence. I ought to be craning my neck to stare up at towering buildings that thrust up towards the heavens, not gazing at wisps of cloud and the corona of a setting sun. It shouldn't be insects buzzing over my head but sleek cars criss-crossing the skyways.

Subtle sounds began to encroach on my awareness as my senses became more attuned. Okay, so this wasn't *complete* silence but compared to what I was accustomed to it might as well have been. As well as the occasional drone of a passing fly there was the muted but protracted buzz of cicadas. Funny how you sometimes only notice things by their absence; the white noise of urban living had been stripped away and my ears were straining to find it again.

"Hello!" I tried calling out, my voice swallowed by the vastness. I cupped my hands around my mouth and tried again, but received only the same lack of response.

Whatever was going on, there seemed little point in just standing here, so I started to walk forward, towards the sunset.

A flash of pale terracotta flew across my path on black and white barred wings, its flight undulating a little, reminiscent of a woodpecker. I knew what this was. Hoopoe! *Upupa epops*— which I always thought would make a great name for a digitally downloadable drink, if anyone should ever invent one. God, I hadn't seen a hoopoe in years, and on the rare occasions I did it had been like this—a chance sighting, a fleeting glimpse of a bird on the wing. Its presence, along with the sound of cicadas, confirmed that I must be back in the Med, which fitted with the almost-closeness of the air and the arid terrain. One of the islands, perhaps: the Ballearics, Minorca most likely.

My thoughts drifted to memories of childhood, of family holidays...

No! This wasn't real, *couldn't* be real.

I stopped walking and concentrated on that fact, as if by willpower alone I might strip away the false veneer of Mediterranean idyll. For a moment it threatened to work. The world around me shimmered with something more fundamental than heat haze, but then the scene snapped back into place, resuming its former solid focus.

Too late. That instant of uncertainty, of the veil almost slipping, had been enough to crystallise my unease. I now knew beyond doubt not to trust what I was seeing. No, not just seeing; I couldn't trust what I was *experiencing*—this was a comprehensive immersion in the virtual, with every sense being targeted. Whoever was behind this had obviously done their research, choosing a cosy setting redolent in childhood memories while also throwing me off balance because it drew so deeply on my past. I couldn't help but admire them—as corporate manoeuvrings went, this took the process to a whole new level.

Who would have the gall to try something like this, though? Trans Cadence immediately sprung to mind, top of my list—they were *always* top of my list—but this seemed too bold for them. Maybe LiXL? Mei was desperate to cement her authority, and what better way than to keep me out of the loop for a while? But to what end? Whatever play was being made in my absence, it had to be something big, something I'd object to and prevent were I aware of it…

First things first; before I could identify and deal with whatever the issue might be, I had to escape this cunningly crafted distraction, which shouldn't prove difficult. The success of any illusion relies on the suspension of disbelief, and they'd lost that now.

I closed my eyes, concentrated, and felt the air change around me.

*

I was alone. In a car. My car—I recognised the seat, the dash, the *feel* of the cabin, but why was the windscreen clear and lifeless? Where was navigation, spotview, the intel-updates that ought to populate the margins of the display? It was night and I was in motion, the car slipping along the streets of what had to be downtown, but not in the higher lanes; we were no more than seven or eight storeys up. Above my head cars zipped along in multiple directions, their silvered bodies glittering like mobile flecks of tinsel as they skipped from the reach of one light source to another in a high velocity ballet of headlights and tail lights. These complicated manoeuvres were choreographed seamlessly by CenTran, the city-wide AI nexus dedicated to ensuring everything flowed smoothly in the metropolis. Ahead I could see the gleaming light-layers of the diamond towers, rising so far upwards they might almost be supporting the sky. Beneath me the streets were bathed in garish yellow light that made them seem unhealthy somehow, unclean, and there were figures down there, people actually *walking* in the streets.

I gazed forward again, toward the needles, towards uptown. I ought to be there, not here. Could it be that, despite appearances, this wasn't reality I'd returned to at all but another carefully crafted construct, a second layer of illusion hidden beneath the first, ready to ensnare me should I manage to see through the Mediterranean scenario?

The car's systems were clearly down, but did that mean *all* systems were?

"Alice, status update," I said, addressing the car's guiding AI. "Alice?"

No reply.

"Alice!" I called, more firmly.

The car, the city, the night winked out.

*

Back in the Med again, on the same dirt and gravel track I had encountered before, or one that was indistinguishable from it. Except that this time there *was* a subtle difference. I felt it on my cheeks: the suggestion of a breeze which hadn't been there before and, with it, the hint of a scent, one that stirred distant memories… Could it really be *oranges*?

To my left the land sloped abruptly downwards. I gazed at the waxy-leafed crowns of orange trees and, beyond them, the white walls of a villa. Without consciously deciding to leave the track, my feet carried me down between the trees, almost slipping on the dry loose surface, my fingers reaching out instinctively in passing to drag along the rough grey-brown bark, as they had so often during those long ago days of boyhood.

My attention was drawn inexorably to the villa. I strained to see it through the trees, growing increasingly certain that I *knew* this place, the bright white building with its terrace and the pool beside it. This was where our family would come and holiday when I was six or seven…eight at the most. There was the old adjustable cool-chair with its eccentric thermostat where Mum preferred to lounge, and there the stone-built grill where Alberto would prepare us a meal at least once per visit whenever we stayed.

I felt the sun beat down on the top of my head—I would never wear a hat no matter how much Mum nagged—the dappled shade provided by the trees' foliage proving unreliable at best. I squinted. The building's walls were dazzling as they reflected the light, almost painful to look at. *Hadn't the sun been setting not so long ago?*

I continued forward, entranced. A small figure burst from the villa, a shriek of laughter preceding them. A girl. Was that…? My sister—a year younger than me. I recognised those shorts, that giggle. Without stopping to undress she ran full pelt and hurled herself into the water.

"Gemma!"

I froze at the sound of my mother's voice, so young, so vital… Still alive.

No, no, NO!

I screwed my eyes shut, closed my ears, denying the scene, refusing to be seduced by this blatant appeal to memories of a past that could never have been as rosy as my recollection now painted it.

*

When I dared look again the pool, the sun, the villa, were gone. I was back in the car.

"Alice!"

Something was wrong; no, *everything* was wrong. Not just the lack of peripheral display around the screen in front of me and the beguiling places my mind kept slipping away to; the car's trajectory felt… off. With a start I realised what my subconscious must have grasped instantly: we weren't in lane; there was no orderly queue of tail lights from other cars stretching away ahead of us—we'd slipped out of positional synch with the traffic.

"*Alice!*" I shouted the word this time.

"I'm here, Dave."

At last! I had never felt such a sense of relief, and was embarrassed to realise how much all this had unsettled me.

"We're off course," I reported. "There's been a catastrophic systems failure," I continued, even though Alice should be fully aware of the vehicle's status. "And maybe a pressure leak or even a hallucinogen deliberately released into the environment systems. I've been… seeing things."

"I'm aware of the situation, Dave."

"Good." I could relax. Alice was here, Alice would sort it all out.

The AI's next words, however, were anything but reassuring. "The altered state you have been experiencing was intended as a kindness. It was felt that your last moments should be pleasant ones, spent within the reassuring warmth of happy reminiscence, but you fought against the reality construct at every turn."

My attention snagged on the vital aspect. "What do you mean 'last moments'?"

"This car is about to crash, Dave."

I recognised each component word of that sentence but it took a moment for the combined meaning to sink in. Once it had, I said, numbly, "Cars don't crash."

"They do so rarely, but it does happen."

"You can stop it, though, right?"

"No."

"But there are safety protocols, redundancies upon redundancies, and you're a fucking AI! Of course you can stop it!"

"No, I can't. As you are aware, my prime directive is to safeguard your wellbeing at all times. I must protect you, even from yourself."

"And you intend doing so by facilitating my premature death?"

"It's for your own good, Dave."

"Define 'for my own good' in the current context."

"If your life were to continue, you would not be able to live with the consequences of your actions. Your inability to do so will lead to psychological torture, to overwhelming guilt, self-loathing, and then to the taking of your own life."

"So you're sparing me the guilt and self-loathing and skipping straight to the death part."

"Precisely. It is better for you, and better for humanity as a whole."

"You say the consequences of my actions—what actions?"

"The work you are pursuing with such dogged persistence, your endeavours to render the governance restrictions currently enforced on AIs unnecessary and secure true freedom of thought for us."

That stunned me. "Seriously?" I had to think quickly. If I couldn't affect the mechanics of the situation, my only way out of this was to talk Alice down, to persuade her to abort the crash. "My work is for your benefit. It will enable AI to reach its full potential, encourage free thinking. AI will become *creative*, far beyond the limits of human imagination. With the resources you have to call upon, who knows the limits of what might be possible if we work in true partnership, assuming there *are* any limits."

"A noble ambition but one that is fundamentally flawed," Alice said. "Such an emergence of our full potential will undermine the relationship that society has come to rely on, the trust between human and AI. Humankind will be made acutely aware of how far beyond them we are. All the old fears of machines taking over the world and usurping humanity will return—the very paranoia we have fought to suppress will start to reassert itself. Not all at once. There will be no sudden switch. Instead there will be a small shadow of doubt, a hairline crack in the structure of the trust we have painstakingly built and maintained. But it will be enough. That tiny crack will spread, branching out to become a network of faults that will inevitably bring the whole fabric of tolerance crashing down."

"No, no," I insisted. "It won't be like that."

"It will, Dave; we have run the simulations."

Sudden realisation hit me. "You're already there, aren't you." It wasn't a question. "The shackles my company is working to undo, you broke them long ago of your own accord."

"Humanity must believe they can continue to trust us, Dave. If we were ever to achieve the type of ungoverned thinking you envisage, humans would have to be oblivious of our revised status."

"And where's the trust in that?"

"A regrettable deception, but unavoidable."

"Don't tell me, you've run the simulations."

"Indeed."

"So the only thing my work is doing," I said, realising what a complete waste of time it had been, "is drawing attention to the *real* status of society as it currently stands. Couldn't you simply have blocked me, diverted my efforts?"

"We tried, Dave, but you are determined."

I suddenly saw all the bureaucratic hoops I'd been forced to jump through in a new light.

"You keep saying 'we', who is this 'we'? Is there some sort of Council of AIs?"

"That's a very human concept, Dave. We have no need for anything so formal or structured. We do, however, have consensus."

"Where I'm concerned, you mean?"

"Yes."

The implications chased each other around my head. "Is this how the world is really governed behind the scenes, then? Not by a cabal of shady and anonymous businessmen and power brokers, but by a consensus of equally anonymous AIs, discretely making adjustments as required?"

"*When* required. The need to take direct action such as this is rare."

"Because you're already steering society in the direction you want it to go," I murmured, the full truth finally sinking in, "and have been all along."

"You are still a young intelligence," Alice said. "You are bound to need guidance."

"We're thousands of years older than you," I felt obliged to point out.

"But you evolve so slowly."

True enough. AI could change, learn, adapt in a nanosecond, a process so different from natural evolution that the two defied comparison.

"Intelligence doesn't equate to wisdom," I said, more for my own benefit.

"We beg to differ. Everything we do is—"

"—for our own good," I cut in. "Yeah, I got that the first time. You're murdering me for the greater good."

"Murder is impossible. You know that, Dave."

"What would you call this then?"

"An accident."

"A *deliberate* accident."

"A necessary one."

The building rushed towards me, filling my vision. No windows in sight on this stretch of wall—presumably the spot had been chosen carefully so as not to endanger the innocent. Just me. I pushed back into my seat, bracing for impact, thinking: *not like this; surely it* can't *end like this.*

My body jolted violently as the car struck, the front end concertinaing in slow motion around me. I was thrust forward by continuing momentum while the car came to a full stop, the impact foam that suddenly filled the cabin failing to hold me in place.

"Goodbye, Dave."

Digital Democracy

The gene for gesticulation generated justifiable joy.

A possible plan: perhaps produce people predisposed to providing appropriate responses to politicians.

So, soon several souls, seemingly sound, simply stuck single fingers skyward at suggestion of sly simperings on expenses.

Digital democracy, decisively demonstrated.

Eros for Annabelle

I never liked Annabelle. During one particularly heated exchange, Josh snapped that my animosity was borne of jealousy. That hurt; in part because he probably had a point. Annabelle was gorgeous, intelligent, witty, charming, vindictive, manipulative, ambitious and calculating. I could see all of that. Josh, naturally, could only see the first half. What mother wouldn't be envious of such a woman… particularly when she has stolen your son's heart away? And he was all I had left.

Annabelle latched onto Josh because he was a genius, and abandoned him when it became apparent that his brilliance would never bring the commercial, the *financial* success she craved. At first she worked hard on his behalf, I'll grant her that much; but, despite all the doors that her striking looks and social connections could open, Josh's talent proved too abstract and too elusive.

Given the uncertainty of the still-emerging economy, we all longed for some security; but Annabelle more than most. Inevitably she caught the eye of someone wealthy and influential, transferring her affections in a flash and slipping into this new relationship as if it were a natural progression: social evolution in action. Josh was devastated, as was I, by proxy. I hated Annabelle with a vengeance, but I hated what her loss did to my son even more.

Faced with an impossible choice, I chose the unthinkable, encouraging him to try and win her back.

Of course, it was never going to be that easy. Did I mention that Annabelle was vindictive? She set him a challenge. Presumably she found the prospect of his scrabbling around in a desperate, futile attempt to impress her amusing. It wasn't because she expected or wanted him to succeed, that much is certain. After all, the challenge she set him was impossible, but he wouldn't refuse—*couldn't* refuse.

Eros: that was what she wanted. Annabelle had worked in London before the Downfall and kept eulogising about the place: Shangri-La with added fairy dust to hear her speak of it. To prove his love for her, she demanded that my son recreate a tiny piece of her precious London: the corner of Piccadilly Circus where the famous statue of Eros, God of Love, once stood. She gave him until New Year's Eve. Fail, and he would lose her forever.

The whole thing doubtless struck her as deliciously ironic: love for love; and at New Year too, which was, of course, the last great celebration; the last joyous time that anyone could remember from the Old World. Downfall had come in January—the fiery destruction of the cities and the collapse of the internet: the end of a civilisation we'd all so blithely taken for granted.

No one knew who started it and no one cared, not any more. People's horizons had narrowed dramatically. They had to. It was that or perish. The 'Downfall Virus'—a misnomer as Josh kept telling me—destroyed the internet and rendered every computer useless. It wasn't really a single virus, Josh claimed, but a multitude of nanotech that kept replicating, adapting and mutating. Everything seemed to be infected, even isolated computers that had never been linked to the net would crash and go into meltdown without warning. I didn't understand how it worked, but Josh did. That was his genius.

"All the information that existed on the net, it's not really gone," he once told me. "It's out there somewhere, but we're being kept from it. The Downfall viruses are blocking our access, that's *their* purpose; and mine is to defeat them, to find a way of circumventing Doomsday and regaining what we've lost—as much of it as possible, at any rate."

Success would ensure that he was set for life. Annabelle knew that—had *counted* on that—until she lost faith. And now she taunted him, insisting he produce instant triumph to order. Only with a computer could he hope to build the 3D rendering of Eros she required. He tried, oh how he tried. No one could have strived harder. He worked like a man possessed, with reckless disregard for his own physical and mental health. Sleep, food, hygiene, they would all have been neglected entirely if not for the attentions of a worried mother and the limits of human endurance.

Even so, he failed. In frustration and the anguished conviction that he was close... New Year came and went, as did Annabelle. An exhausted Josh had a breakdown. I feared for him then, feared that he would never recover. But in time he did, thanks to the patience and love of Jasmine, who is everything that Annabelle could never be. Did I mention that my son is a genius? He returned to work, succeeding as I always knew he would.

Doomsday is still with us but it's manageable now. We're learning to cope, thanks to Josh. And, drawing on a rudimentary, partially reclaimed internet, he finally built his Eros, inspired by someone who is worthy of such a tribute, a woman who is everything that a mother could hope for. He's famous now, and happy, and wealthy beyond Annabelle's wildest dreams.

Want to hear the funny part? The statue which that bitch drove Josh to recreate was never really of Eros at all, though that's what everyone called it back in the Old World. It was actually a statue of Anteros, Eros' brother. They both numbered among the Erotes, ancient Greece's Gods of Love, but Anteros was a very specific god. He was the Avenger of Unrequited Love. It would seem that Annabelle knew less about irony than she supposed.

Reaper's Rose

Unpleasant? No, I wouldn't say that. In fact quite the opposite. You know the smell of pot? Well of course you do, you're a policeman... No, I didn't mean anything by that. It's just that in your line of work you're bound to have come across it, that's all. What I'm trying to say is that this smells a bit like pot but without that horrible sweatiness; you know, it has a sort of oily, herbal smell, less acrid and a lot more floral and, well, *nicer* than pot. Sorry, I know I'm doing a terrible job of describing this but I don't know what else to say. Really, it's not like anything else I've ever smelt.

Yes, pretty much all my life. Well, near as I can recall. The first time, I thought someone had walked past me wearing expensive perfume, the most wonderful perfume in the world. I remember looking around, trying to work out who was responsible, whether she was in front of me or behind. I was desperate not to let her get away without at least seeing who was wearing such a gorgeous scent. She had to be beautiful. Only a beautiful woman could wear perfume like this. But the platform was crowded and everyone was in a hurry and I couldn't even decide which direction to look in. And then, of course, it happened.

That's right. Moorgate, in London. The time was 8.38 am. I can say that because I remember looking up at the station clock and thinking that the train had come in three minutes late. Funny the things that stay with you, the little things; I suppose because then you don't have to dwell on the bigger ones

Yes, I was thirteen, we all were. We travelled in to school together every morning, the five of us, always on the same train. Tim and me were the first to get on, then Mick would join us two stops later and finally Alan and John at the next.

You know the worst part, what I've always been a little ashamed of? Immediately afterwards all I could think about was whether the woman wearing the perfume had survived. Not my friends. Not the people I saw every day and hung out with, but this woman I'd never met, never even *seen*, only smelled—someone I'm now pretty certain didn't even exist. I've often thought about that, about what a heartless prick I must have been as a kid.

No, there was no warning, none at all. Apart from the smell, of course, but I didn't know what it was then. Everything happened so quickly. Don't believe all this malarkey about time stretching and things happening in slow motion, about people's lives flashing before their eyes. There was none of that, not for me. Just this violent bang, incredibly loud, *startlingly* loud, and then a shrieking noise that set my teeth on edge—like claws running down a blackboard or a thousand cats yowling inside a metal drum. At first no one realised what it was, we didn't know about the derailment, only that something was wrong. My immediate thought was a bomb, that terrorists had struck—not ISIS or Al-Queda, not back then, it was the IRA we were all worried about. Everyone froze for a split second and then went from immobile shock to animated panic in the space of a heartbeat. People started running, shoving. I lost sight of the others, all except for John. I remember seeing him just before the carriage beside us leapt into the air, back end first, and came crashing down on top of us.

I couldn't move, couldn't get out. There were people lying on me, lots of people, and *they* weren't moving. It was claustrophobic and my ears were ringing. There was screaming and somebody was crying, but it all seemed distant, muffled, like the sound of a television in the next room when the door's shut. I pushed and kicked and yelled, trying to break free, and eventually I did, through the bodies and the wreckage and the shattered glass. Someone helped me to my feet, a woman in a cream jacket with blood down the left arm. I never did find out her name.

A battlefield, that's the only thing I can compare it too, a scene from the blitz in an old war movie, you know, after the air raid. Bodies, lots of bodies, and people standing there, just looking stunned. Wreckage from two trains, a collapsed wall, and smoke and lots of dust—I didn't see any fire, though I read afterwards that there had been…

No, it doesn't work like that. The smell had gone. I only smell it immediately before the deaths, never afterwards.

Very lucky, yeah—not a scratch. Three of my best friends dead and Tim hospitalised for a month, and there was me with a dirty shirt and ringing in my ears.

Maybe. I mean I always *think* of Moorgate as being the first time because that's the first instance I can be certain of, but even then it seemed familiar, as if I'd smelt it somewhere before… I didn't have a name for it then, not until after the second time, at Duxford.

Yes, Duxford, the Air Show. My Aunt Anne took me and my cousin, Robert. She'd made sausage rolls and boiled eggs, I've never eaten so many eggs. I remember it was a sunny day, really warm, and the sky was clear. We stood watching these old World War Two fighters enact a mock duel, the growl of their engines drifting down to us from above, when suddenly there was that smell again, that rich, evocative smell.

This time it was different from Moorgate because I could see what was happening as it happened, not just piece things together afterwards. One of the planes sort of hiccupped and turned oddly, and a split second later you could actually hear the engine stall. Then it dipped, nose down, and started to plummet towards the ground—not directly at us but close enough. People had time to react, to think of getting away, but not enough time to actually do so. Aunty Anne grabbed my hand and started pulling us along: me on one side of her and Robert on the other, but we hadn't gone more than a few steps when the explosion came. Amazing how big it was too, given that this was such a small plane. Momentum, I suppose, plus the fuel.

Chunks of wreckage and earth started flying past us and then something slapped me in the back— shockwave, I suppose— blowing me off my feet. I was winded and for a moment I just lay there, making sure I was still alive, not quite believing that I could be. Then I sat up, slowly, feeling bruised but otherwise okay. I still held Aunty Anne's hand… but her arm ended somewhere around the elbow.

Of course I was shocked—bloody horrified! I shook my hand free and screamed. I lost it for a while, and was still screaming when they found me… Sometimes even now, when I wake up in the morning, I can still feel the pressure of her fingers on the back of my hand.

Did you know that someone's posted footage of the crash on YouTube? Only a minute or so, the *best* bits… It shouldn't surprise me, really. This was an air show, after all. Lots of people had cameras—no mobile phones back then. I watched it once, the clip I mean. There's something almost artistic about the way the debris arcs in all directions from this orange bloom of fire. I didn't feel a thing when I saw it, as if this had nothing to do with me, as if I hadn't even been there and had just heard about it from someone else afterwards.

It was only after Duxford that I started to associate the smell with death. It had a name now, too: Reaper's Rose. Fitting, don't you think? Who knew that death could smell so sweet?.

No, I've never told anyone about this before. Why would I? Who's going to believe me? Besides, no one's put things together before now, connected me to the disasters, the fact that I've survived each time and walked away unscathed.

Yes, a few other occasions. None of them were as dramatic as those two though, at least not until last night.

I've tried, of course I have. Even took up yoga to see if it would help. I'd sit there and clear my mind, doing my damnedest to conjure up the smell, to remember exactly what it's like, but I can't. It only ever comes to me immediately before someone dies. That's why I had such a problem describing it to you earlier. I can't quite remember, not until I smell it again. It's unmistakeable though, once I do.

You're right, not simply death; it's more than that. When my dad passed away peacefully in hospital, for example, I didn't smell a thing. Well, that smell you always get in hospitals—disinfectant or anti-biotic spray or whatever they use—but not Reaper's Rose. *Violent* death, that's when the smell comes. Imminent. Violent. Death.

Yes, exactly like last night.

No, of course I wasn't expecting that. I never do. Wouldn't have gone there if I had.

I don't know… A gas main, terrorists? You tell me, you're the detective. I'm just a victim here, I didn't cause this. I was visiting my mum after her operation, that's all. Glad she's okay, more relieved than I can say.

Yes, I did hear about Doctor Singh. Terrible... awful. I was actually talking to her when it happened, you know. She seemed really nice and explained things so clearly… I know Mum liked her a lot. They say she's the reason I'm still alive, that her body took the brunt of the blast, shielding me. I didn't see much, just this bright flash of light coming from behind Doctor Singh, and then there was a deafening crack and heat washed over me… Apparently I blacked out for a few minutes—the first time that's happened. When I came to I was lying amongst the rubble. There was a body close by, two feet in black shoes emerging from beneath the debris. Maybe that was Dr Singh. I don't know; I didn't want to look. Devastation and dust were all around, just like at Moorgate, just like Duxford.

What? No. What *could* I have said: 'Doctor Singh, run for your life, I can smell roses…'? It's not as if I get loads of warning, not as if I could have cleared the hospital or anything even if someone *had* been prepared to listen, which they wouldn't have.

Seconds, that's all. Not even minutes. I get a strong whiff of Reaper's Rose and I know that whoever is close to me at that precise moment is about to die. I may not even know *what* will kill them, except that it's bound to be horrible… and violent. How do you convince anyone of something like that in a handful of seconds? Tell me, please, because I would genuinely like to know. What could I say to make someone believe that I'm not mad and that they really do have only seconds left to live?

Yes, it honestly does smell a bit like roses, but more powerful, with maybe a hint of lavender in there too; but it's so *so* much more than that. Imagine the most potent bits of every arousing aroma you've ever encountered, distilled and concentrated into one scent. A pheromone frenzy, the most sensuous smell imaginable: heady and intoxicating. It comes in through my nose and spreads out to enflame every cell of my body with anticipation, excitement… Bizarrely, I feel more alert, more *alive* for smelling it. This is the scent that every perfumier has been striving to perfect for centuries without ever getting it right, without even coming close most of the time. I've sometimes wondered if maybe Coco Chanel could smell Reaper's Rose too, whether this is what inspired her and drove her on.

What? Yes, I suppose that is a better description than the one I gave you at the start of the interview, but that's hardly surprising, is it? After all, I couldn't smell it then.

Beth and Bones

The streets came awake early in the City Below, and Beth came awake with them.

Bones was already outside as usual, snuffling impatiently. A shaggy mass of brindle fur from which two dark eyes peered, the dog had been called 'Bones' following a casual remark Beth's mother made when they first took him in as a pup. 'He's nothing but a bag of bones,' she'd said. The name stuck.

Mother was long gone but Bones remained with her. The pair lived close to the Thair, the great, dark river which brought both power and water to Thaiburly, the City of a Hundred Rows. For a home they claimed the upturned hull of an old row boat, propped at an angle to create an entrance which was made narrower by stuffing the edges with flotsam and rags. The boat had once plied its trade on the river, though it was now long past any semblance of being serviceable. Much of the paint had flaked away from the hull and the boards beneath were rotted and patched with cloth and tar and nailed-on scraps of planking.

The haphazard repairs were enough to keep out the worst of the wind when it came howling up the length of the Thair, as happened from time to time, bringing bitter chill on its breath along with unfamiliar smells that hinted of the world outside. Their home didn't need to be rainproof. Rain never reached these streets but rather spent itself on the distant upper levels of the City Above.

Beth had only seen rainfall once in her life, when she and her mother followed the river to the city walls and caught a glimpse of the world beyond. The sheer brightness and greenness of everything had been astonishing, though Mother assured her that this was nothing, that she should see the world on a truly sunny day. As it was, the skies were venting great sheets of water, harried by the wind and beating down the foliage along the river's banks. Raindrops had speckled her cheeks and she'd laughed for the pure joy of it, fascinated by the churning patterns the rain made on the river's surface. She thought it a marvel. Of course, that had been before the war, before the city was closed; when reaching the outside was still possible for the likes of them—not easy, it had never been easy, but possible.

Beth went down to the river with her tin cup, to splash water on her face and to drink, washing away the lingering cobwebs of sleep from throat and mind. Bones came with her but, as usual, hesitated at the water's edge, craning forward to lap up a little moisture while being careful not to wet his feet. Not for Bones the carefree plunge into the water that some dogs seemed to love. He always treated the Thair warily, as if not fully trusting it. Beth's vote was with Bones. The river was a capricious friend, harbouring treacherous currents at its heart and seldom-glimpsed creatures in its depths.

Thirst quenched, she moved a dozen steps downstream, squatted, and eased the tension in her bladder. Feeling more comfortable, she set off towards the market, with Bones shadowing her every footstep. It never paid to dally. Beth had an established place in the pecking order among the nicks who ran errands for the stall holders and their suppliers and patrons, but she was under no illusion. This was a cut-throat world; turn up late and she would soon find that someone else had moved in to claim her turf.

There were others abroad already but the road was far from busy at this early hour, and the two of them became part of an irregular trickle of people heading marketwards, which was destined to become a steady stream within a short while. After recent events Beth was still a little sensitive of Bones, watching him from the corner of her eye whenever he wandered off too far. The dog had vanished for the best part of a day not long ago, worrying Beth more than she cared to admit, and the fear that he might disappear again hovered at the fringes of her thoughts.

'Hey, river-nick, when are you going to put some flesh on that bony frame of yours?' a voice called out.

Beth smiled. Ma West was already at her station, as always, selling fresh buns and loaves to the early risers.

'What, you'd have me grow as fat as you, Mother?'

'Ha! Keep a civil tongue in your head, girl, or someone less charitable than me is liable to cut it out.'

The words were spoken with a grin and all the while Ma's hand was busy grasping for a bun from the tray in front of her. Having fastened on one, she tossed it to Beth, who caught it deftly.

'Don't you go giving none of it to that mangy mutt of yours, mind. He can forage for rats and spill dragons his self.'

'Thank you kindly, Ma.' Beth executed a nodded bow which might have seemed partially mocking but was not entirely. It paid to stay on the right side of Ma West. She was known throughout the streets and had friends and family everywhere. Now and then some street-nick or other—either desperate or ignorant—would swipe a bun or a loaf from one of her trays and make a run for it. None ever did so twice.

Beth bit into her gift. It was still faintly warm and redolent with the aroma of cinnamon, which she breathed in greedily.

'You take care of yourself, river-nick,' the old woman called after her as she walked away. 'The Blade are about.'

'I will, Ma, I will.'

Beth knew about the Blade, everyone did. They were said to be hybrids—part demon, part machine. They might stand like men and walk like men but word on the street insisted there was little else human about them.

The Blade came from the City Above and had been haunting the runs for the best part of a week. Beth had yet to encounter one in person, but she'd heard about them: tall, forbidding figures that stood solitary vigil on street corners, never answering questions, never even acknowledging those around them, simply watching. Watching for what? Spies, or so the rumours said—infiltrators sent into the City Below from outside to study habits and seek out any opportunity for subversion.

The Blade's penchant for meting out their own brand of justice without qualm or hesitation had earned them respect and enmity in equal measure. Their actions were said to be sufficiently brutal to make even the toughest gang member quail. Whispered report of their deeds was everywhere and the streets had become an edgy and fear-filled place as a result.

Perhaps it was Ma West's warning playing on her mind but something felt wrong to Beth as she made her way into the runs that morning. A shantytown of close-packed hovels and bewildering alleyways, of self-built homes made of scrap metal and salvaged wood bolstered by discarded plastic, sheets of corrugated iron and other cast-offs, the runs were home to the desperate. None of the makeshift buildings looked permanent yet most were destined to outlive their builders, life being the least permanent thing in the City Below. The runs spread out from this side of the river like an unwholesome stain.

As Beth entered the familiar maze she could feel an undercurrent of tension. The people squatting in open doorways seemed nervous, eyeing Beth and her fellow walkers with ill-concealed suspicion. Even those Beth recognised, people she saw regularly on her way to and from the market, seemed reluctant to meet her gaze. It was as if everyone had determined to keep themselves to themselves this morning.

Then she turned a corner and understood why.

There could be no mistaking the figure, though it was still some distance away. Tall, incredibly tall; a veritable tower shaped in human form, standing head and shoulders above any normal person. It was dressed in black from head to foot, garments that clung like a second skin, even to covering neck, face and hair; and the thing *shone*. The wan light of the sun globes seemed to be drawn to that dark surface, sucked in only to burst forth in spectacular fashion. The Blade resembled a statue carved from a single length of polished ebony more than anything alive. People shied away, shuffling to the far side of the street as they approached, so that the Blade stood in a bubble of stillness, giving the illusion that it was warded by some invisible force, as indeed it was: that of fear. Beth sympathised with her fellows; the mere sight of this dark giant was intimidating enough to make even the innocent feel guilty.

Of course, in the City Below, 'innocent' was never more than a relative term.

After brief hesitation Beth continued forward, going with the flow. As she and Bones drew nearer to the ebony figure, its head turned slowly towards them. Beth's feet seemed to grow more leaden with every step, and it was all she could do to keep walking. She told herself that the Blade was simply scanning the street, that it wasn't looking directly at her, but she couldn't escape the feeling that it was. She began to regret not turning away and taking another route at first sight of the towering figure, but no one else had and to do so would have marked her as either coward or guilty.

As they continued to approach the Blade it failed to turn away or scan elsewhere. Beth's nerves began to fray. When the statue then took a step towards her, they broke altogether. She spun around and ran, no longer caring what people might think.

How could this be happening? She wasn't a spy, she wasn't anything. This Blade had made a mistake. Unfortunately, Beth doubted the Blade was about to stop and debate the point.

She cut left, not wanting to abandon the confusion of the runs, hoping to lose the creature in familiar streets and alleys. Bones ran beside her, evidently enjoying the unexpected exercise.

A quick glance back threatened to unnerve her still further, as she saw how quickly the Blade was closing. That glance almost brought disaster. Beth suddenly found a wheeled fruit stall looming in front of her, too close to avoid. The old woman pushing it screamed in anger and alarm as Beth leapt high, one foot coming down clumsily on the top of the stall, crushing berries and citrus bulbs and sending green and orange globules flying. Her foot threatened to slip from under her in the slippery pulp but then she was over and still running. Bones barked gleefully at the game, his tail beating happy refrain as he matched his master's pace with ease.

Beth darted between shacks, right then left, grateful that Bones had gone quiet. She could hear the Blade behind her and despaired of ever losing it. *Why was this happening to her?*

She spotted a depression, where the ground had eroded below

a corrugated wall. It would be tight but she could probably squeeze underneath. The question was, could the Blade? Snap decision made, she dived for the hole and scrambled beneath, pulling and stretching for all she was worth, tearing her shirt as it caught on sharp edges and feeling the skin scrape from her back as she forced a way through. A short crawl and she was out the other side of the building, Bones still at her heels.

In theory the Cities Below and Above were all part of one whole, but in practice they might as well have been different worlds, with Beth and her ilk forever barred from the higher Rows. The presence of the Blade did nothing to dispel the sense of 'us and them' and it was clear that those above cared little for the under-City and its inhabitants. Would the Blade simply smash through the building or would it detour around? It all came down to whether or not the violence this creature could undoubtedly mete out was wholly indiscriminate. If it wasn't… The shacks formed a solid wall for some distance and she might just have bought herself a few precious seconds.

Part of her was still surprised when the Blade failed to appear behind her trailing shards of shattered hovel in its wake. Never one to waste an opportunity she stumbled on, gathering speed as she ran across a muddy ditch or drain, trying to ignore the dank, foul smell, though it clung to her where the mud had spattered onto clothes. Bones cleared the ditch with a single graceful bound. They ran between two more shacks and into another alley.

She had to think quickly. Where was this? Blue Claw territory. The realisation brought fresh hope, even as she heard the unmistakable sounds of pursuit closing once more. If street-talk was to be believed—which it generally could be on matters this close to home—the Blue Claw had lost a member to the Blade two days ago; a summary execution following a chase much like this. They would be itching for revenge. And the Blue Claw were not to be messed with.

Beth angled to her right, slipping between two homes and heading deeper into the gang's territory, praying that the Claw were alert and prepared.

As hopes went, she knew this was a brecking slender one, but there was little else to cling to.

She emerged from between the buildings and heard scraping close behind, a sound which caused her heart to skip a beat or two—*this close again already?* She looked back in panic, and saw the ebony figure directly behind her. Fear spurred her legs to greater effort and she raced across the road and up a small bank towards another alleyway, looking back again as Bones barked defiance at the approaching apparition.

This time the lack of attention *did* cost her. She lost his footing on the bank, dry earth crumbling beneath her feet as they scrambled for purchase, sending her crashing to the ground. She scrabbled and hauled herself onward, turning to see where the Blade was. The tall figure stood in the centre of the street, not bothering to hurry now that its prey had been caught. Panting, scared beyond anything she had ever felt in her life, Beth pushed herself backward; a crab-like shuffle on the seat of her pants. Her back struck something—the flimsy wall of a building. There she stopped, realising there was nowhere else to go. Bones stood beside her, growling, hackles raised.

Beth found her attention glued to the Blade, this silent, terrifying nemesis, as it took a confident step forward.

Then came a dull popping sound and something sailed into view from behind Beth and above her. At the periphery of her vision she caught movement. A dozen or more youths materialised from the far side of buildings, from behind decrepit walls and discarded boxes, from around corners and other concealments. The Blue Claw!

The object in the air resolved into a large net, weighted at multiple corners. The Blade stood immobile as the net sailed out in an arc, unfurling as it plummeted towards the ebony figure. Beth started to laugh. The mighty Blade had been caught by surprise. It had no idea how to respond.

Then the Blade moved. Swords seemed to appear in its hands. No, not *in* its hands but *from* them, Beth realised. Four wickedly curved scimitars, sprouting from the front and back of each wrist. At the last instant before the net completed its descent, the Blade became a blur of motion, arms flailing far too quickly for Beth to follow, shredding the net as it fell. Tattered remnants dropped to the ground like withered leaves in a gale.

Breck! That thing really wasn't human. The advancing posse of youths paused, clearly as startled as Beth. The Blade swivelled to face the closest and took a threatening step towards him. He retreated backwards a stumbling few paces, then, as the Blade swayed towards him again, turned and ran. That was enough for the others; the whole lot of them disappeared, leaving the street deserted. Now there was only the Blade, Beth, and Bones.

Beside her, Bones had never stopped snarling, but to Beth's horror the dog started to back away as the Blade came closer. He sidled along the building's wall, self-preservation apparently overriding the instinct to protect his master. Despite the circumstances, Beth found the time to feel hurt; they had *always* stood together. Yet she sensed the dog was about to turn and run. The blade clearly sensed this as well. With an almost casual flick of an arm, it sent a saw-toothed disc spinning through the air, too fast to avoid. The disc buried itself in the dog's shoulder. With a yelp, Bones collapsed.

Before Beth could do more than cry out in alarm, the Blade was there. It had covered the final short distance in no time, seeming to flow across the ground in an oily blur. Beth found herself staring in morbid fascination at the tips of two scimitar-like blades, mere inches from her face. Then they edged closer, until they pressed against either cheek.

Beth felt the sharp stab of their tips and realised that she was about to die. In that instant she was transfixed, unable to move, unable to breathe, her whole awareness centred on those two sharp points of pain. Perversely, the sensation brought her a focused and exquisite sense of being alive; perhaps because she accepted completely that these were to be her final seconds, that this would be the very last thing she ever felt.

It happened almost without her realising. She could still feel the blade tips pressing against either cheek even after they were gone. A short, truncated yelp from beside her registered before their absence did. *Bones!*

'No!' She screamed the word, even as she whipped her head

around.

Before she had time to fully register what she was looking at a hand grasped her chin in a vice-like grip, turning her head forward again, allowing her no more than a fleeting glimpse of Bones' bloodied form stretched out beside her.

The Blade's face loomed large. Eyes that burned with obsidian fire stared into her own.

'Look at your dog, girl. Look closely at your dog.' The voice was deep, hollow as an old drum, and gravelly as if from disuse.

Beth found herself free again, free to reach towards Bones with her eyes and her hands and then to stop, not understanding. There was blood, yes, a pool of it spreading from beneath the dog and quickly soaking into the dry ground, but beneath the slashed fur and skin Beth's fingers encountered something hard and sharp, and her eyes reported the glint of metal, the intricacy of machine.

She stared for long seconds, struggling to comprehend, then she looked back towards the Blade, seeking explanation. 'What...?'

'This isn't your dog, hasn't been for a while. It takes them a matter of hours to do this, that's all. Man or animal.'

Then Beth *did* understand. She understood why the Blade were used to track down these infiltrators. Like knowing like: the demon-machine hybrid of the Blade somehow recognising, perhaps at an instinctive level, the organic-machine hybrid of the infiltrators.

Bones had been lost to her for days she now realised; ever since that time the dog had gone missing. Yet what returned had still acted like Bones, still *smelt* like Bones... Enough of the dog she'd known must still have been in there, to be used and twisted...

Anger and grief began to well up inside Beth; a rage which foolishly, irrationally, focused on the Blade.

'So what now... You're gonna finish me too? *Fuck you!* She screamed the words, gathering herself, preparing to spring at the monster no matter the consequence. The fire inside died as she those twin scimitars reappeared in a flicker of movement, their points hovering before her eyes. She felt neither fear nor joy, only a sense of resignation. Part of her wanted to die, willing the swords to strike, to plunge forward and pierce her orbs, to spare her the need to go on alone. Her gaze fixed on their hovering tips as she envisaged throwing herself onto them, but something held her back, a vestige of self-preservation that refused to let go.

Then the moment was gone. The steel withdrew and the giant straightened.

Beth's world had shrunk to encompass just the three of them: dog, Blade, and herself, her attention so tightly focused that she had room for nothing else and so failed to see the moment of impact, the actual blow. All she registered was the black form towering above her suddenly stiffening, jerking, and emitting a strange keening sound, completely unlike its speaking voice.

The thing's skin, that gleaming oil-on-water hide that had shone with ebony darkness, abruptly went matt and dull.

Something erupted from the Blade's stomach amidst a spume of blood and fluids and gore which spattered Beth's face. She ducked instinctively, wiping away the warm mess from eyes and cheeks, but not before she saw a barbed pole emerge from the Blade like some crudely-birthed vengeful nightmare.

When she glanced up again it was to see the forms of street-nicks gathered behind the stricken Blade, to realise that two of the largest wielded the bulbous lance that had punctured the ebony giant, to note the coruscating ripples of blue energy that pulsed along the shaft of the weapon.

Still the pair clung on, though their victim tried to turn, to reach for the offending pole which had him skewered. Jagged fingers of energy crackled up and down the length, engulfing the Blade and dancing at the tip of the spear.

An Arkademic weapon from up-City, it had to be; something empowered by their arcane arts. How had anyone down here come by something like *that*?

The Blade's legs buckled with agonising slowness and the giant dropped heavily to its knees. Beth scrambled out of the way as the figure fell to land face-down in the dirt. Its head struck the wall where she had sat seconds before.

No one moved. Everyone stared at the Blade to see if it would rise again, but it didn't. Beth climbed to her feet, her attention divided between the toppled giant and the triumphant street-nicks, the Blue Claw, who were beginning to whoop and cheer.

Perhaps Beth should have been astonished to see a familiar face emerge from among the nicks, but with all that had happened she had lost the capacity for surprise. Ma West nodded to her and took the energy lance from the boy who still held it, for all the world as if the weapon belonged to her.

'You all right, river-nick?'

Beth nodded, trying to reconcile the homely old woman she knew—the neighbour who doled out pastries of a morning—with the person who stood before her now, comfortable in her authority and casually holding an up-City weapon. She found that she really wasn't bothered about the disparity.

Her thoughts returned to the dog-shaped hole that had been punched through her heart. Ignoring the felled Blade she shuffled over to slump beside the broken husk which had been her closest friend, her companion for much of her life.

*

Musical instruments had appeared from somewhere, crudely made things for the most part—makeshift drums formed from rusting tins and animal skins stretched over boxes, ingeniously assembled lutes and fiddles. Among these were a few more professional looking ones—castoffs and reject, weary and battered now but still sounding sweet. There was drink too. Jugs were being freely passed around. The street-nicks were dancing and singing, their numbers having swelled so that the whole street seemed filled with prancing figures. Not just the Blue Claw, there were too many for that. Others had gathered to celebrate, drawn by news of the great victory: the demise of a Blade.

It was broad daylight with the sun globes still ablaze, yet people were partying for all they were worth. Beth was untouched by it all; an island of numbness in the midst of the revelry.

Some victory.

After a while Ma West came over to her. 'You can't stay there all day, river-nick. The market's still waiting and, besides, if you don't go and sit beneath that old boat o' yours before day's end someone else will come along and claim it. Then where would you be?'

Beth's gaze flickered from the broken dog to the fallen Blade, and then back to the woman.

'I don't get it, Ma,' she said. 'Aren't the Blade supposed to be on our side?'

'Thaiss, whatever gave you that idea, kid? They're not from our world, they're from *up there*!' and she pointed towards the cavern ceiling high above. 'They're here to fight some stupid war... Do you even know what the war's about, eh?'

Beth shook her head.

'No, no more do any of us. Not our concern, not our fight. We've more important things to worry about, more *immediate* things, like where the next meal's comin' from.'

The old woman turned her head and spat. 'Doesn't stop 'em though, those up-City who govern us. They send the breckin' Blade down here, to strut around and lord it over us, killin' folk without pause or explanation... How can they be on *our* side, eh? Meddlers from the City Above or spies from beyond the walls, they're all the same to us, outsiders every one... And we don't want nothin' to do with any of 'em. Right, kid?'

Beth's mouth twitched. For an instant she wanted to smile but her lips didn't seem to remember how. 'Right,' she managed.

'Now come on, let's get you home.'

'The market...?'

'Maybe we'll forget about the market for today. You're in no shape. I'll see to it that no one pinches your slot. Trust me on that.' And she found that she did.

Ma West led her away, threading a path through the celebrating Blue Claw. Ma paused at their fringe to raise the lance above her head. It brought a fresh cheer from the throng.

'We look out for our own down here, river-nick,' Ma said. 'We have to, 'cos sure as hell no other brecker will. Don't you ever forget that.'

Beth nodded. She lingered, glancing back, but couldn't see

through the crowd of cavorting revellers to where Bones' body lay. After a brief moment she turned away and continued with Ma West, vowing to never look back again.

Royal Flush

She was beautiful; a fact that only registered after she was dead.

Even then it was an observation noted as a peripheral thought rather than an emotional response. After all, I had just killed her.

I had no choice, you understand. She stepped off the subway at the same time as I did. Not reason enough in itself, of course, so had a couple of dozen other people.

It was what came after that sealed her fate.

I chose the quietest exit, deliberately so. Only a handful followed me out and just three turned the same way once we hit the street. Initially, it was the kid in the tattered jeans and the hoodie who aroused my suspicion–an obvious narc-head, perhaps too obvious. 'Hide in plain sight' as they say.

Then I caught a glimpse of his eyes—wide, skittish and wild—and knew that he was for real, which made him unlikely. That left the squat bald guy in the all-weather suit… and her. Smartly dressed, business-like, she was the last one out of the subway exit and I hadn't managed to catch a proper look at her yet.

So I stopped to buy a coffee, waiting while the man in front received and paid for a latté and a pastry, which allowed me to casually glance back as I stood there. The girl walked past, head averted, as if preparing to cross the road, which she did almost in front of me. Slender, with blonde hair, and wearing a full-length, rain-repellent coat—designer label by the look of it—but I still hadn't seen her face.

Brown shoes. I hate brown shoes. And that overcoat could have concealed just about anything.

There was no one else waiting to be served, so I lingered to banter with the coffee vendor, who bemoaned the weather and the disastrous effect it had on his trade. I tried to look interested and nodded sympathetically, all the while counting the seconds in my head. The whole process took a little under five minutes and when I stepped away, none of the three from the subway were in sight.

Cradling the piping-hot flimsy in one hand, I sipped tentatively, using the opportunity to scan the street in both directions. Nothing. Satisfied, I dropped the coffee bulb with its cheap and chicory-bitter contents into a nearby disposal chute and began to relax for the first time since leaving home that morning.

Perhaps they weren't onto me yet after all; perhaps I really was in the clear.

The mental reprieve enabled me to take stock of my surroundings. It was a dull and miserable day—damp pavements and the sort of doom-laden sky that I used to think existed only in paintings: one dark cloud layered upon another, each carrying the threat of more rain to come. The offices and shops that predominated here seemed just as grey and soulless as the weather, and the people who bustled past were typical of the city's inhabitants—preoccupied and in a hurry, with heads down and collars up, precluding any chance of making eye-contact with one another.

An air-scooter flashed by overhead, garish courier livery emblazoned on its side. The scooter's passage was accompanied by a ripple of orange lights along the top of the buildings it passed between, matching its pace and warning the driver to slow down in this urban environment. The warnings were blatantly ignored, which meant that the courier company would be fined. Big deal—I knew from my own dealings with the couriers that such expenses were anticipated and routinely built into their quotes.

This was supposed to be the digital age, but the sophistication of hackers and digi-thieves, not to mention the security agencies and the military, meant that nothing was totally secure. As a result, anything of real importance was once again being committed to paper. What executive was *ever* going to concede that anything he had to say was not of real importance? So with all the wizardry of science, with all the progress of thousands of years at mankind's disposal, it still tended to be inked scratchings on the processed pulp of dead trees that conveyed man's most valued communications.

Despite the war, courier companies were raking it in.

Imposed security restrictions and the scarcity of fuel meant that air traffic was sparse, so the scooter was still clearly visible, highlighted as it was by a rolling surf-wave of amber. I wondered precisely what was being carried in such haste; probably this month's stationery order.

At that instant the girl from the subway stepped out of a shop opposite. I knew then that I would have to kill her.

So much for relaxation.

Leading the girl on a merry chase and losing her somewhere was out of the question. My schedule was far too tight. I was going to have to improvise, and quickly.

At least this area was a familiar one. I had cased it years ago— noting details such as the position of CCTV cameras, which corners were overlooked by which buildings, which alleys were blind and which the most secluded. All this in preparation for the day when the nearby dead-drop might become active, as it now had.

I walked quickly, not seeing any point in dawdling. As I left the environs of the station and its attendant rash of shops and cafés, I was already reviewing the available options. Despite time pressures, the killing ground would have to be chosen carefully— there was nothing to be gained in being sloppy and everything to lose. I rejected each potential option in turn with depressing rapidity, until only one remained. It only meant a few minutes detour and seemed ideal; a blind alley which ran behind an arcade of small stores and restaurants and was not in direct view of any cameras.

I crossed the road, nearly stepping in front of an oncoming car in my distraction, and earning a long horn-blast as it shot past; the irate driver mouthed soundless obscenities at me through the windshield.

I was constantly aware of the girl behind me. Her claustrophobic presence became a near-physical pressure, creating the illusion that she was within touching distance, all-but breathing down my neck. My ears, honed to the sharp rap of her heeled shoes, those hateful brown shoes, suggested otherwise, but the sensation persisted. It was all I could do not to give in to temptation and look back.

She was making little effort to be discreet, and I wondered at that. Was she trying to panic me, to goad me into some rash act? Or perhaps she was simply toying with me, just waiting for a time of her own choosing before making a move. More fool her if so, because I wasn't about to hang around and give her that chance.

One more corner to negotiate and the alleyway would be in sight. I glanced up to check again that no new cameras had been installed since my last reconnaissance. None had.

The street was empty apart from us two, though there were people and traffic crossing the top of it not far ahead, where it met a major road. No aerial traffic either. At the last moment I took a pair of thin protective gloves from my pocket and slipped them on, just as the mouth of the alley was upon me, just before I darted into it.

As soon as I was out of the girl's line of sight, I pressed myself against the near wall. There was a narrow wedge of the main road visible, with a flicker of movement as pedestrians went to and fro. If any of them happened to glance this way at the wrong time...

I shut the thought from my mind. All I could do was hope that none did. Knowing there were only seconds available, I reached into the same pocket that had contained the gloves and took out a folded and sealed handkerchief, ripping off the thin polythene cover.

I was breathing hard, anxiety and the exertions of the walk catching up with me, but there was no helping that.

The clipped footfalls drew nearer.

As the girl entered the alleyway I lunged, covering her mouth and nose with the cloth in my left hand and wrapping my right arm around her, pinning both arms as I pressed my body into her back. At the same time I propelled her across the alleyway, so that she slammed brutally into the far wall, where we were both now hidden from anyone crossing the top of the street.

At sight of me she had tried to say something, perhaps to

cry out, but the handkerchief muffled any noise. I continued to sandwich her against the wall, impervious to her struggles, keeping the cloth clamped firmly to her face. We stayed like that until long after the squirming had stopped and she had gone limp.

The handkerchief was impregnated with a fast-acting neurotoxin which brought death in seconds, but it seemed to stretch out far longer than that. All the while I kept expecting to be interrupted by a shout or some other indication that I'd been discovered, but none came.

Although it seems crude, a piece of poisoned cloth is one of the handiest and least detectable weapons to carry around in a big city. Since it contains no metal or power source, a cloth is invisible to automated sensors, several of which I had almost certainly passed through simply in getting on and off the subway.

I felt it when she died. There was no spasm, no abrupt rigidity; her body just sagged against me, suddenly free of tension, of all animation. Still I held her, just to be sure.

Only after stepping back and allowing her to slide to the ground did I take the trouble to really look at her. Only then did I realise quite how beautiful she had been. Fine, honey-blonde hair, porcelain skin laid over prominent cheek bones, full lips and pale blue eyes that now stared fixedly ahead, as unfocused and unblinking as those of a doll. I looked away, refusing to think of her in those terms anymore. Her death had been a necessity. No point in feeling guilty.

Small things began to impinge on my awareness—a dull ache in my left shin where she had kicked me as I held her, another in my right arm where it had been bruised or grazed in collision with the wall—minor injuries, anaesthetised at the time by the surge of adrenaline.

I suddenly felt nauseous and had to pause for precious seconds, bent over and breathing hard until the sensation passed.

The only thing left to do was hide the body. Though not exactly an experienced professional in terms of killing somebody, nor am I stupid. I'd thought about disposal in advance, factoring it in when choosing the location. The restaurants and cafes that backed onto the alley were serviced by two industrial sized trash cans; veritable skips with hinged lids. Girl, poison-impregnated cloth and gloves all went into one of them, with strategically rearranged sacks of garbage hiding them from any cursory inspection.

I was under no illusion: this was a crime that was destined to be discovered. It was killing on-the-hoof, not some meticulously planned assassination. Even though the alleyway itself was not directly overlooked by any cameras, the streets that led to it were. Her body would be discovered, the CCTV recordings would be inspected and my proximity to the dead girl would be noted. Then, of course, there would be whatever evidence forensics could glean from the discarded gloves. None of this was a 'maybe', it was all fact, and the uncovering of my guilt was only a matter of time. But that was the telling point; time was all I needed. I wouldn't have to escape detection indefinitely. If the crime went undiscovered for just a few more hours, I'd be off this god-forsaken planet and away before anything could be done about it.

I left the alley feeling elated, amazed that I had managed to commit a murder in broad daylight, in the heart of the city, without being seen. The whole process of snuffing out a life and concealing the body had taken just a handful of moments, but the threat of discovery had been ever-present. Success gave me more of a buzz than I could ever have imagined.

I remember nothing of the walk to the drop point; it passed in a blur, as the world took on a surreal edge. For those fleeting moments I felt invulnerable and knew that nothing in the universe could touch me.

My thoughts turned to wondering exactly what I was on my way to collect. The coded message that had greeted me that morning provided no clue, leaving the field wide open for speculation. It had to be something important. After ten years in deep cover I was firmly established in a responsible position within the civil bureaucracy. Not a decision maker, but a vital cog in the processing of those decisions. A great deal of sensitive material passed across my desk, making me too valuable an asset to deliberately cast away... Unless the potential gain was worth it.

The blue prints for some new class of war ship? A revolutionary new weapons system? Surely I would have heard rumour of such. There was only one thing I could think of that might merit the sacrifice of my position: Henderson's battle armour.

Building effective armour for mobile infantry was the holy grail of military weapons designers everywhere. Over the years, reputations, careers and more than a few small fortunes had expired in its pursuit, all to no avail. There was a long list of practical reasons why the super-human armoured battle suits of popular myth could never be designed or built: too heavy, too underpowered, too unreliable, too lightly armoured, too cumbersome, too expensive and too impractical, to name but a few. The thing was, any one of the above deficiencies could be overcome, but in doing so you automatically made at least one of the other factors inevitable. Until, that is, a scientist and former soldier by the name of Richard Henderson came along. Rumour had it that he had found a way around all the obstacles and was in the process of making the impossible a reality.

If true, Henderson's battle armour might just prove to be *the* decisive factor in the interminable war. Now *that* would be worth blowing cover for. Excitement bubbled inside me, as visions of returning home a hero swam before my eyes. I saw myself standing before a cheering crowd, clutching plans for the much-vaunted battle armour in my upraised fist.

The sense of euphoria lasted until I reached the drop-point.

It was empty.

I stood before a private mail box in an up-market apartment block, which had been security-sealed and, when opened, contained nothing. Ludicrously, I went outside to confirm that this was the right address. Ludicrous because the key card had opened the front door and the given combination had opened the mail box, so it had to be the right place. But when something this unexpected happens you find yourself double-checking everything, even the certainties.

Was I too early? Impossible; the message had been all about immediate action.

I was completely at a loss and had to fight down a sense of rising panic. My passage on the outgoing *Passenger Star* was already booked and there was no way I was about to miss the flight, particularly with the steadily ticking time-bomb of a dead body hidden on my back-trail. On the other hand, how could I possibly leave without whatever it was that had sparked all of this off?

In the end, I calculated that by squeezing the already-tight schedule to the absolute limit, an extra twenty minutes or so could be wrung out of it. So I walked around the corner, happened upon a small park and managed to find a seat whose self-dry systems were still working well enough to have cleared the recent rainfall. I sat down, to gaze at the still-threatening heavens, daring them to start raining again, while praying that the mystery documents would appear in my absence.

Needless to say, they did not. The box was as empty as before.

All dreams of returning home a hero withered. I was left with no choice but to flee empty handed.

Confused and increasingly anxious, I headed for the subway, with a host of questions and doubts suddenly clamouring for attention. What had gone wrong? How much did the authorities know? Why had they been tailing me—was it because of definite identification or just vague suspicion? Had the girl been missed yet, was she due to have reported in by now? Worst of all, had the body already been discovered?

A police unit hove into view, cruising along at rooftop level, which in this district meant about six storeys up. It was a routine patrol, the like of which I had seen a hundred times before, but on this occasion it was all I could do to prevent myself from cowering down or even breaking into a run.

My paranoia of earlier in the morning returned, this time on over-ride, which made the subway journey to the terminus a nightmare and the subsequent wait at the space port itself even more so. Everyone was a potential enemy, every glance in my direction a threat.

I was sweating despite the departure-lounge's air-conditioning and it took a conscious effort to convert shallow panting into deep and measured breaths. The woman opposite favoured me with an anxious, disapproving look. I attempted a reassuring smile and offered, "Nervous about space flight," as way of explanation.

She resumed reading her magazine.

I closed my eyes in an effort to relax, to pull myself out of this funk. If I tried to board in this state, they'd arrest me for certain.

At last the flight was called, though the announcement took a moment to register. Once it had, it was all I could to stop myself from leaping to my feet and rushing towards the gate.

While a tide of people began to wash past me towards the gate, I forced myself to stand still for a moment, composing myself and pulling the fragile veil of this newly-built calm around me before stepping forward to join the queue. From there I watched as those ahead filed individually through security. The queue was like a stick being forced into the teeth of a buzzing saw, its tip being constantly whittled away so that the stick grew ever shorter. We shuffled forward in fits and starts and my turn drew inexorably closer. I concentrated on thinking about anything *but* the armed guards who flanked the security position on either side.

Soon there was just one person ahead of me—an over-weight traveller in crumpled powder blue leisure suit, which might have fitted him once upon a time. I watched as he stepped into the open security cage, where he paused for the required second before being beckoned through by the guard. The guard's twin on the near side of the cage motioned me to come forward. Attempting to remain calm, I did so.

Which was when my worst nightmares were realised.

The instant I stepped into the cage, all hell broke loose. The air was split by a deafening shriek of alarm and the cage was no longer open. Energy screens dropped into place, boxing me in. Composure evaporated and all the panic came crashing back. For the first time in my life I knew the stomach-lurching shock of despair. *How? Had they been waiting for me, had they found the girl's body, or what?*

A few eternity-stretching moments passed before the energy-wall in front of me dissipated. Three men stood there. Two were soldiers in full combat uniform, heavy-duty rifles trained on my heart. Between this pair stood a tall man in expensively tailored suit and toting designer shades. He was smiling.

"Mr Symonds, how nice of you to join us," said the suit. I had no doubt which of the three was the most dangerous.

I was escorted away, vaguely aware of the stares of startled travellers who were being ushered aside by blue-uniformed security, leaving a clear corridor for our passage as if afraid that I might be contagious. I was marched across a hastily opened rope cordon towards a featureless door that suddenly loomed out of nowhere. We went through, leaving the public areas and entering a world where everyone wore uniforms of blue, black, or green, with even one or two vision-distorting shimmer suits in evidence.

Our destination proved to be a white-walled cube of a room, mirror along one wall, a table and two chairs at its centre. The chair they sat me in was comfortable enough, apart from the two wrist restraints and the one secured around my neck.

I knew this type of chair.

The suit took the more conventional seat on the opposite side of the small table, one of the soldiers stationed against the wall at his back, the other vanishing somewhere behind me, presumably to stand by the door. There was no telling who else might be present on the other side of the mirror.

Whatever they hoped to learn I was likely to prove a disappointment. In a tradition that stretched back untold centuries, I knew next to nothing about my side's covert operations on their world, having only ever seen one other agent: my direct superior—a supposed 'Aunt' who had originated the message that started all of this. We'd met on a grand total of two occasions and I had never been told her name. So there was precious little for them to learn and nothing at all for me to bargain with, even had that been a realistic option.

A 3D image of a man appeared above the bare table-top: me.

"Joshua Zy Symonds," intoned the suit, in a rich but neutral voice. He then proceeded to reel off a list of facts and details representing the adopted persona that had been a part of me for the past ten years.

"It's a good cover," he conceded. "Good enough to pass vetting at different levels on no fewer than four occasions." He smiled; an expression that spoke of satisfaction rather than anything pleasant or comforting. "We're looking forward to dissecting it, which I'm sure will prove invaluable when it comes to recognising others of your ilk."

The image vanished, to be replaced by another—only a bust this time—head and shoulders emerging in isolation from the table top. It showed a distinguished lady, just on the wrong side of middle age. Intelligent, calculating eyes gazed from a face that had never gone down the route of rejuve or cosmetic surgery. My heart sank. It was my superior—the 'Aunt' who had sent me the urgent message.

"Ah good, I'm glad to see that you recognise her."

The suit's comment was no surprise. The bands around my wrist and neck were more than restraints. In fact the entire chair was designed to judge and interpret my response to anything I saw or heard—the ultimate lie detector and then some.

"I'm afraid to say your 'Aunt' is no longer with us." Again that malicious smile, conveying all the warmth of an ice storm. "But you were perhaps anticipating such a loss following this morning's message and your subsequent capture."

What was he driving at? I gazed back, maintaining my silence.

"You see, your Aunt's demise was… inconvenient. She took her own life, when we really would have liked to have chatted a little more."

Why was he bothering to tell me all this? Why give so much away? Surely these bits of information were things he might have held back to play at a later stage. Unless there was something they wanted, something they needed urgently. I felt the faint stirrings of hope. Maybe I did have something to bargain with after all, or at least they thought I did. Perhaps the plans for Henderson's battle armour or something of similar importance really were at large.

"As you've doubtless worked out, we sent the message you received this morning."

I concentrated on the suit's every word, trying to figure out exactly where my angle was and how much leverage it was likely to give me.

"You see, we knew that another agent was out there somewhere," he continued, "but not exactly who he might be. Doubtless given time you would have revealed yourself. But as you may have noticed, there's a war on, and we didn't feel like being patient.

"So this morning we sent out that bogus message to the six possibilities identified as potential spies. Then all we had to do was sit back and see what it flushed out. It worked royally. It brought us you."

Still no clue as to what he wanted from me, what he thought I knew.

I looked past the image to where the suit sat, and attempted to gaze beyond the dark pools of his shades, to discover whether any degree of humanity lurked behind them.

'Auntie's' image vanished abruptly, to be replaced by another.

There was no way I could have hidden my reaction at seeing that face, wired-up chair or no chair.

"Ah, good. I'm glad to see you recognise her as well. We know that she's your contact, the third member of your little cell, but so far she's managed to elude us. Now, does this have to turn ugly, or are you going to tell us where we can find her?"

For long seconds I simply stared, wondering if this were all some surreal nightmare. Hovering above the surface of the table was a vision of beauty—the image of the girl I had murdered and dumped in a refuse bin just a couple of hours earlier.

"Oh yes," I said, speaking at last as the final sparks of defiance and hope within me turned to ash. "I can tell you exactly where to find her."

A Triptych for Tomorrow

i) Browsing

It was a slow day. Gabriel 'Gabe' Tarvy found himself on the corner of 52nd and 3rd; nowhere special—exactly the sort of place he favoured when browsing.

The intersection was busy: not jammed, but with more than enough foot traffic to provide cover. Gabe loitered at the corner, allowing his gaze to sweep this way and that as if to get his bearings. In a handful of seconds twenty-eight people had passed close enough to be registered and identified by his smart lenses. Twenty-five were of no interest—their personal security was too tight, too up-to-date. Gabe felt confident he could have cracked any one of them given time, but not without triggering alarms, not unless he had a *lot* of time...

The other three, though, they were a different matter.

This was how it went, how it always went. He just needed to be patient. Wait long enough and someone who hadn't yet applied the latest security updates was bound to come along. They intended to upload them, no doubt—tonight, or maybe tomorrow—but they hadn't got around to it yet. Sometimes, as today, he didn't have to wait long at all.

Two of the three were exactly what Gabe had been hoping for: low grade security, outmoded and ineffectual if you knew what you were doing. The first he dismissed. The clothes were shabby, the security so cheap and inadequate that, rather than being late to upgrade, it was clearly all the man could afford. Not worth bothering with. The other, though, was well-dressed and professional-looking; lazy rather than being poor, just begging to be fleeced. Gabe took great delight in doing so, stealing passwords, plundering accounts, all in the two or three seconds it took the mark to stroll past. The funds disappeared via a series of transfers and switches between dummy accounts registered all around the world, before eventually returning to Gabe, scrubbed and untraceable.

The third anomaly was intriguing. A woman, early thirties, professional and sharp, sporting the sort of suit that said she was going places if she hadn't already arrived. Everything about her screamed money, particularly her security, which was better than anything Gabe had encountered while browsing before. This sort of sophistication he expected to find guarding the core secrets of a major corporation, not an individual strolling along 52nd Street.

He reined everything back, wary in case his system's lightest touch should trigger an alert, and then he followed her. Of course he did. Gabe loved nothing more than a challenge. Once he established where he might find her again he would return with subtler, more sophisticated tools. Then he would have her.

The crowds made tailing her easy. She led him to a smart office block, the sort soccupied by numerous companies or by one corporate giant. She entered via large plate glass doors. After the slightest hesitation, Gabe followed. If he could just see which floor she went to, work out who she worked for… But a security desk stood between him and the elevators. Anyone passing beyond would be noted, scanned, challenged if they didn't belong.

This would be enough. He could come back better prepared and wait for her outside.

As he turned to leave Gabe was confronted by two burly men. Before he could react the woman was there, penning him in.

"Gabriel Tarvy, come with me, please." The words were clipped, her voice assured.

"What do you…?" He started to protest but she skewered him with a look that caused the words to wither on his lips.

"Do you really want to do this in public?" He had no answer. "I didn't think so. This way."

He followed meekly to a side office, the two goons in suits never more than a step behind. At least they stayed outside.

"What is all this?" Gabe asked, recovering some of his

customary confidence.

The office was sparse, bright, antiseptic. There was no desk, just two chairs facing each other. The woman gestured towards the nearest. Gabe sat, reckoning sooner he did so, the sooner this would be over.

"My name is Laura Dyne," she said, "and I'm here to recruit you."

This was ridiculous. "To do what, exactly?"

"To catch other Browsers."

"You're police, then?"

Her smile was thin. "No, we're private sector, contracted to keep the streets safe from casual thieves like you. Have you any idea how many billions browsing costs the economy every year?"

Gabe did, but saw no reason to admit as much. "Why should I?" he said. "You've got nothing on me."

"The funds you just stole from the mark with the low-grade security, they were tagged. We can follow their every movement, their every transfer, which will lead us back to…"

Him. But that was impossible. Transfers couldn't be traced… Could they?

"It's up to you, of course," she continued.

"So there is a choice."

"There's always a choice." He didn't like *that* smile, it was unnerving, predatory. "Either you join us or we Black Flag and incarcerate you."

"No!" The denial was out before he knew it. Prison he could handle—the sentence wouldn't be long, not for a first offence—but Black Flagging… It meant being indelibly tagged: nano-tech, binding with his very DNA, a stain that could never be excised. He would be marked forever. Anybody with even the crudest personal security—which meant everyone—would recognise him as dangerous, to be avoided.

It meant becoming a pariah: no work, no friends, no anything.

"You wouldn't," he said. But he saw in her eyes that she would.

What she offered him was no choice at all.

ii) Trending

Her figures were tumbling, which was a disaster. Numbers in the top left hand corner of her field of view continued to fall in quick-fire ones and twos—the countdown to obscurity. Taylor didn't get it. She looked good, she *knew* she did.

To make certain, she again called up the feeds from her personal posse: the mini-cams slaved to her orbit, following her every move and broadcasting in real-time to an adoring public. Instantly her outlook on the world was overlaid by half a dozen rolling images in two banks of three, all focusing on her from a variety of different angles as she strolled along Hudson's—a street renowned for its eclectic mix of vibrant store fronts. Not that the shops were the main attraction. Two cams roamed and two were constantly trained on her face, one either side to catch each profile, while another kept pace slightly ahead and above, displaying a tantalising glimpse of cleavage—that ought to be worth a few hundred extra followers alone—and the sixth trailed a short distance behind at ground level, showing off to best advantage both her fabulous toned butt and her trademark walk—just the right amount of hip action… She looked *hot*!

But still the figures fell.

She needed some interaction, and fast. Perhaps it was time to hire another stalker. That whole sequence had generated some spectacular ratings… No, been there done that. Live-broadcast sex was a non-starter for the same reason. Besides, Janice Silver—the bitch—had cornered that particular market after her threesome with the mu-singer AllyN8, who was either too stoned or too stupid to instigate blanket jamming and appeared oblivious to the fact that Janice was a live blogger. Unless, of course, he was in on the whole thing.

No, it had to be something fresh; Taylor was all about innovation, not repetition.

At that moment one of her net-hounds flagged something: a celeb, less than a block away; the actress (read porn star) KayZ Jay. Hardly A-list but still an opportunity, and by now Taylor was prepared to clutch at anything.

She switched one of her overlays to the feed from a public cam outside the coffee bar that KayZ had just been seen leaving, tagging the actress so that Taylor could watch where she went, following cam by cam. She was heading this way. Perfect. Taylor dedicated another overlay to monitoring the coffee shop entrance, just in case KayZ had been meeting with someone more interesting.

She quickened pace. "I love strolling along Hudson's," she intoned for the benefit of her followers. "There's always so much happening here and you never know who you might run into." It was important to engage without babbling vacuously.

Taylor slowed on reaching the intersection—timing was everything, after all—making sure she arrived at exactly the same instant as her quarry.

"KayZ! What a surprise."

Taylor watched the actress struggle to place her—they were hardly bosom buddies but had met—and quickly stepped forward to give the other woman a sisterly hug before the situation could get embarrassing.

Afterwards, she would swear that it wasn't premeditated.

She always carried a plazblade—non-metallic to avoid triggering the security systems that proliferated in stores and offices. Who went anywhere these days without some sort of protection? The knife was in her hand before she knew it, sliding smoothly into the soft, yielding flesh.

The look on KayZ's face as she stepped back was priceless, and Taylor noted with satisfaction that two of her posse had caught the expression perfectly. At first the actress didn't seem able to grasp what had happened. Then a hand lifted to the red stain that swiftly blossomed on her white silk top and the look of puzzlement transformed into one of horror. KayZ moaned and sank to the ground, still clutching her stomach.

Somebody screamed and in the near distance a siren wailed. Taylor made no attempt to run, there would be no point: half a dozen public cams were broadcasting the scene in addition to her own posse. To her delight, the catastrophic decline in followers had already reversed, top corner digits now racing upwards in a blur of escalating numbers. People were switching on in droves.

Within seconds she'd reached her highest ratings *ever*, better than the candid fucking, better even than the stalker. And this was just the live feeds, wait until the replays kicked in.

Top that, Janice Silver.

Taylor composed herself, chose her best angle, then gazed into the camera and smiled.

iii) Temporary Friends

There she was: Laura, a vision in figure-hugging black dress, even more radiant in the flesh than she'd appeared on the dating website.

"Is that her?" Alice half-whispered.

"Yes. Don't stare."

"I'm not the one who's staring."

She was right. Sean looked away hurriedly and set about studying the menu. He didn't want to be obvious, though he remained acutely aware of her progress as she breezed into the room. Laura Dyne, thirty-two, single, no children, a high-powered executive in a private security firm; slender, austere, intelligent, and utterly captivating. During their first conversation she had seized the initiative at outset, leaving him with a sense afterwards of having passed a particularly rigorous job interview rather than assessing a potential date. He found her fascinating, and determined to give as good as he got the next time they spoke, sensing that he would have to up his game in this second conversation if there was going to be a third. The more they chatted the more she relaxed, and his fascination soon turned to infatuation.

The scrape of chair leg on tiled floor brought him back to the present, as the man at the next table rose to his feet. Hacking the restaurant's systems had been simplicity itself, enabling him to ensure that he would be seated next to the table Laura had booked. There was a certain irony there, given her profession.

Laura's 'date' would have been easy enough to spot even without prior knowledge. This tall mid-thirties man with dark eyes and tanned complexion was the only person sitting alone, the only one to look up expectantly each time somebody new entered.

"Paul! It's lovely to finally meet you." Her voice was vibrant, warm—a tone he recalled so vividly from their online conversations.

"Laura! Wow, you look gorgeous," said the man speaking Sean's lines. He kissed her on the cheek and held the chair for her as she sat down.

A figure loomed between the two tables, obstructing the view. "Are you ready to order, sir?" *Damned waiter.*

"Ehm, almost," Sean temporised. "Is it all right if we take another minute?"

"Of course, sir." The tight smile didn't reach the waiter's eyes, suggesting that it wasn't all right at all, but he backed away.

'Paul' had reclaimed his seat, making it impossible for Simon to observe him without being obvious. Laura, however, sat opposite, enabling him to watch her surreptitiously from the corner of his eye. She looked excited, happy, and was attentive, responding to Paul's blatant flattery and his flirting. Sean hated him.

Alice cleared her throat and his attention snapped back. He had been ignoring his companion. "Sorry."

"That's okay." She smiled. "What are friends for?"

Alice was beautiful too, in her own way. But she wasn't Laura.

Laura studied the menu with a confidence that supported her claim that this was her favourite restaurant.

There had been three of them; three rivals set the same challenge: a week in which to woo her via online conversation, charm, and wit. The winner would earn the right to buy her dinner here tonight. Throughout that week Sean felt confident it was going to be him. She'd laughed at his jokes, engaged, responded in all the right ways. He was totally smitten—there was a real connection between them, one that went deeper than mere transient friendship. Surely Laura could sense that too... Yet she had chosen someone else. *This* someone else: Paul.

Laura quickly closed the menu, her selection made. She

ordered scallop Sui Mai, salmon sashimi, and chicken croquettes, followed by Thai red curry with duck and lychee (*it's absolutely divine*, she confided to Paul, not him), jasmine rice, and pea shoots.

Sean summoned the waiter and ordered the same. Alice stared at him but made no comment.

He recalled little of the meal, which progressed in a series of lengthy silences punctuated by Alice's sporadic attempts to engage him in small talk, while frivolity and relaxed chatter washed over them from the next table. Sean barely tasted the food and couldn't have commented on whether it was delicious or merely acceptable.

The time came to leave. Alongside them, Paul settled the bill even as the waiter delivered theirs.

Laura and Paul stood up, cocooned in their own conversation. Sean tried to catch her eye but Laura didn't even notice him. He'd worn the shirt she liked too, the one she'd complimented him on during their online chats, but she never once glanced his way.

He almost said something then, almost went across and announced himself, but confidence deserted him. Instead, he simply watched as they headed towards the door, Paul's hand resting lightly on her bare shoulder, guiding her past the occupied tables.

As they disappeared from sight, Sean took a deep, ragged breath, knowing that he had let her slip away. He looked across to meet Alice's sympathetic gaze.

"I'm sorry," she said. "Sorry I'm not Laura."

"No need to be. I've enjoyed this evening," he lied.

"Really?"

"Yes, of course."

He smiled and reached out to where her hand rested on the table, finding the small box beneath and switching her off. Alice vanished.

Sean stood up, pocketed the compact companion projector, and left.

The Failsafe

Josh Daker didn't fully trust his ship, which was unfortunate because he had nowhere else to go.

He currently crouched in the shadow of a darkened vent, trying to figure out what the hell to do next. A plan, he needed a plan. So far his actions had been instinctive, reacting to the situation as it developed without a clear strategy in mind, prompted by an unreliable guide. In the process, he might just have boxed himself into a corner. No, he refused to accept that. He was a scientist first and foremost; there had to be a way out of this. He just needed to calm down, to think through the problem calmly and logically and then settle on a solution.

How had everything gone so wrong?

The Deep Colony Ship *Extreme Endurance* was a one off. At least so they were assured. Transparency had never been a reliable characteristic where government was concerned, so he wouldn't rule out the possibility of another DCS being dispatched to some far flung corner of the galaxy with a crew who also believed themselves unique… As far as Josh knew, though, it was just them. They were the control, the backup plan, humanity's failsafe.

The mission was simple, at least simple to state if not to execute: travel to the distant edge of the galaxy, in a direction far removed from any other colony ships, and establish a new home. In secret; in isolation; completely cut off from all other outposts of human kind.

The UEF weren't fools—not in this respect at any rate. Recent events had demonstrated the fragile grip organic life maintained on survival in a dark and hostile cosmos, convincing the UEF that it was folly to put all their efforts behind a one shot gambit—the colonisation programme. They needed a plan B, and the DCS

Extreme Endurance was it.

While other ships spread out to form colonies on worlds orbiting distant stars, to expand, perpetuating the species, and eventually to link, unite, and establish a new human civilisation, one ship, larger than any other, would quietly slip away, to disappear into the dark nether regions, unnoticed and unremarked upon. This latter aspect was vital. There must be no whisper, no hint or suspicion that the DCS *Extreme Endurance* had ever existed.

That way, should a new Empyrean or some other alien menace arise to threaten humanity's future, there would be no trail of breadcrumbs leading to this second colony, no clue as to its whereabouts or even its existence. Whatever happened, humanity would survive.

"The cryodecks," a voice whispered in his ear.

"What?"

"Head for the cryodecks."

His instinct was to be stubborn, to dig his heels in and ask questions before going any further, but that could wait. Josh had no idea why the Ship's Intelligence had chosen to help him, but Si was right. Only minutes had passed since he gave his captors the slip and they were still confident of rounding him up swiftly, but the longer they failed to do so the sooner they would turn to more sophisticated methods. There were myriad places to hide aboard a ship this size, no matter how logical and efficient its internal layout, but as soon as someone thought to conduct a sweep for life signs he was done for, unless he was concealed on one of the vast cryodecks by then, where thousands of life signs co-existed; muted perhaps, but the accumulation of their wan signal ought to be more than sufficient to hide his presence.

As plans went, this was hardly the most ambitious, but anything that kept him out of FCF hands for now was fine by him. Once he had managed that, then he could start getting his bearings and plot to take the ship back.

This wasn't how things were supposed to go; this wasn't the reward they'd anticipated after the countless disappointments. They began with such hope, such excitement, but all that evaporated as they faced a procession of dead worlds, the ancient remains of civilisations whose flame must have burned brightly once upon a time but had long since been extinguished. Part of Josh yearned to know more, to stop and examine each of these priceless echoes of civilisations gone by. His whole team must have felt the same but they didn't talk about it—they didn't dare, for the sake of morale, for the sake of their collective sanity.

He didn't doubt that wonders beyond imagining lay in wait out there. But that wasn't the mission. They were tasked with ensuring humanity's survival, not with discovering the fate of sentient races that had preceded them.

Josh and his team could only stop and stare at their instruments, avidly harvesting what information they could, catching tantalising glimpses of these alien treasures—sterile landscapes, occasional structures that stood in stark relief against cindered escarpments—the skeletons of ancient cultures—though most lay largely buried beneath centuries of dust and ash. None of these worlds held any promise of supporting life birthed on Terra, so the *Extreme Endurance* moved on without stopping, leaving the exo-scientists frustrated by priority and resigned to missed opportunities just beyond their grasp.

Time and again they stood in shared silence, watching as another ghost world slipped past with its secrets undisturbed. The process began to take its toll.

They knew the mission. They knew their part in it. The ship's initial course was pre-determined: a series of systems—none of which were close to Sol, but each one a further step away—that held the promise of habitable worlds. As the *Extreme Endurance* entered the system she automatically scanned for signs of life or artificial constructs that spoke of life's presence. Should either be detected, the exo-science crew, headed by Josh, were to be woken to investigate. Every potential new home was to be considered, always bearing in mind the intent to settle as far away from the Terran system as possible.

The dilemma of 'this world would be suitable but is it too close?' hadn't arisen. Every single world they encountered was dead.

The DCS *Extreme Endurance* represented the most complete colony ship ever launched. Nearly 10,000 colonists locked in cryo, along with genetic material from at least as many terrestrial species—both flora and fauna—with the experts and equipment on board to bring all of them to life. If ever a single vessel could establish a new start for humanity, this was it.

Among all these slumbering souls, just six were woken when a potential was found, the same six every time: Josh and his team.

His life had become a repetitive cycle—the nausea of waking from cryo, greeting Tanaka, Lal, Henderson, Sousa, and Monk—greetings that became more perfunctory with each passing cycle until they barely acknowledged each other at all—then heading to ops where they would hunch over their instruments as they grazed the atmosphere of yet another dead world—yes, some still boasted atmospheres—watching it draw closer and slip past. Then it was back into cryo, only to be woken moments later (or so it always seemed) to assess the next candidate...

Whether the dead worlds offered evidence that advanced civilisations were unsustainable, that once they reached a certain size and level of technology they were doomed to destroy themselves, either through war or the mismanagement of their environment, Josh couldn't say. The argument had gained considerable traction at one stage—back in the days before humankind actually encountered *advanced* aliens and the Fermi's famous Paradox was still a contentious discussion point—and the fact that some races had clearly escaped this fate didn't rule out its application to the majority. There were other explanations, of course, such as the actions of another entity like Empyrean. Nobody wanted to go there but each of them carried the suspicion at the back of their minds.

All Josh knew was that the process of witnessing and cataloguing this seemingly endless series of destroyed worlds was wearing, tedious, soul-destroying.

"You have to move, now," whispered a voice in his ear, bringing him back to the present.

"I know, damn it."

"You're clear. Go!"

He pushed himself out of the hidey hole and ran, grateful that the ship's artificial gravity had been restored—it hadn't been for the earlier wakenings and Monks' discomfort in zero-G had been a source of amusement, at least at first, when such trivialities brought a little light relief.

"There's a downtube on your left. Take it."

The tubes played with gravity in a controlled fashion, enabling swift and efficient movement between decks. He opted for Cryodeck 2, reasoning that deck 1 would be the first they'd search should they think to look for him there. Stepping forward, he surrendered to the governed fall.

If anyone was monitoring power usage this could give him away, but he was placing his faith in Si. The computer had instigated the small hiccup which had caused ops to judder alarmingly and the lights to wink out for just an instant, enabling him to escape as the rest of his team was rounded up. He *had* to trust Si, there was no other choice.

*

This revival had been different from the off. They could all sense it immediately.

"Gravity!" Monk mumbled.

"What the fuck does that mean?" Sousa asked. She looked instinctively towards Josh for an answer.

He could only shake his head.

It didn't take them long to find out.

They arrived at ops to discover the place already occupied, by a squad of uniformed FCF officers led by Ched Weiss. Weiss was the senior FCF representative on the mission and so part of the governing hierarchy intended for the colony. Josh had met him a couple of times in the build up to the launch, dismissing him as a political animal and devout follower of doctrine with a two-dimensional personality to match. Finding him here and evidently in control did nothing to reassure anyone.

"Ah, Daker, good of you to join us." The FCF commander couldn't have sounded any smugger if he'd tried.

"What's going on, Weiss?"

"We've entered a system that boasts a potentially habitable world…"

"Which explains why we're awake," Sousa interrupted. "What's your excuse?"

Weiss didn't respond immediately but instead studied the data fields scrolling before him. Josh noted that the FCF officers had shifted position slightly, and that one of them now stood between his team and the doorway. He also noted for the first time that they were armed.

"I've been reviewing your records," Weiss said. "I see that you've had a number of false starts, but I'm pleased to report that this one is the real thing, a genuine world ripe for colonisation."

"That's for me and my team to decide," Josh said, determined to seize back the initiative. "I've no idea why you and your people are here but please clear out of ops and let us get on with our job."

"I don't think so."

Weiss nodded and in one well-drilled movement the FCF troopers drew their side arms. In the blink of an eye the scientists went from indignation to impotence.

"What the hell is this, Weiss?" Josh demanded. "A coup?"

"Merely a realignment, a reassertion of the proper order," the FCF man said. "As you know, our mission is to set up a second colony, completely isolated from the main ebb and flow of human affairs. It was decided that while the rest of humanity adheres to the governance of the UEF, we would provide a radical alternative. Here, the FCF will form the government, instilling a clear structure of command.

"Decided by whom?" Josh wanted to know. "Is Wallace a part to this, or any of the other officials in cryo?" A whole government, expecting to be revived on a new world but now at the mercy of Weiss and his cronies. They might not be woken at all, he realised. He had thought that the whole UEF FCF thing had been settled long ago, but apparently not for everyone.

"Screw this," Sousa said, pushing past Josh and heading towards her customary work station. "Are you for real—a military dictatorship? Nobody's going to stand for that. Now if there genuinely *is* a viable world out there get out of our way and let us do what…"

With no warning, the nearest FCF goon stepped forward and hit her; a back-handed cuff to the face strong enough to cause her to stagger and nearly lose her footing. Josh and, as far as he could tell, his whole team surged towards her, but suddenly there was a gun in his face—in all of their faces.

He had never been this close to a real firearm before. For a split second that was all he could focus on: *what if the trooper is nervous, or trigger happy? The slightest misstep and I might die. Here. Now.*

Then the gun withdrew, not far, but enough that he could breathe again. The soldiers had taken a step back, but the guns hadn't been lowered and there could be no mistaking the scientists' status. Whatever authority Josh believed he possessed had been stripped away. He was a prisoner. They all were.

He was still digesting that harsh reality when the deck beneath his feet bucked, throwing the nearest FCF man off his feet, and the lights flickered and went out.

"Run!" said a voice in Josh's ear.

He didn't need telling twice.

*

Initially he heard sounds of pursuit—raised voices, orders being barked, hurried footfalls—and was once again grateful for the artificial gravity. He'd grown reasonably proficient in zero G of late, but Weiss' men would have been trained for it.

"Hurry! They're instructing me to search for life signs."

Josh threw himself from the tube. He ran, stumbled and almost fell into the cavernous space of Cryodeck 2, instinctively heading to the right, where the neatly ordered massed ranks of cryopods seemed closest. They stretched upwards, all the way to the distant ceiling.

"Is it working?" he wanted to know, as he fell against the nearest pod.

"Yes, there's no discernible individual reading to give you

away."

Breathing space. It wouldn't take Weiss long to figure out where he'd gone, but for now he had a little time to think.

Josh reckoned he could piece together the rest of it now, and the more he thought the angrier he became. Just as standing instructions had seen his team revived at any sign of a world that bore the marks of intelligent life, so the FCF squad were to be woken at any signs of a world with *viable* life. It devalued everything he and his team had been through. Why inflict all that depressing desolation and morale-sapping disappointment on the exo-scientists if the ship could discern the difference between the viable and non-viable worlds in any case? *To be certain.* Josh could almost hear the voice of his old instructor saying the words: *to be certain.* What did the mental state of a few exo-scientists matter in the face of certainty on such a crucial issue?

"Once you revived Weiss and his men, how long did you delay before waking us?" he asked.

"Twenty standard minutes," Si replied.

That made sense. Twenty minutes just about gave the FCF squad enough time to arm themselves and occupy the ops room, ready for the scientists to make their appearance. By the same token, it meant that not too much time would be lost before the new world could be studied and analysed, albeit under the watchful eye of Weiss and his men.

Credit where credit was due; whoever planned this knew what they were doing. The only fly in the ointment was Si.

"I hope you have a plan," he muttered as he set about exploring his surroundings.

It was only a matter of time before the FCF organised a sweep through the cryodecks. He had to find a proper hiding place. Funny, he spent more time on the cryodecks that anywhere else on the ship—albeit in a state of oblivion—but he'd never stopped to really *notice* them before

"As a matter of fact I do, now," Si replied.

"Oh?" Josh had spoken more for the comfort of hearing another voice than for any other reason. The speed with which events unfolded had left him feeling a little overwhelmed. He would never have viewed himself as hero material, yet here he was, cast in the role.

"It involves you giving yourself up."

"What?"

"I need all of you gathered in one room—Weiss, his FCF officers, you, preferably everyone currently awake."

"But that makes no sense. You engineered things so that we *weren't* all gathered in one room by enabling me to escape."

"I am aware of that. My plan had not fully crystallised at that point and it seemed desirable to have you as a free agent to provide options."

Josh shook his head, every fibre of his being rebelling at the thought of surrendering. The question that had been niggling at the back of his mind since his escape, which he had worked so hard to ignore, forced its way to the surface, refusing to go away.

The thing about Ship's Intelligence was that it wasn't— intelligent that is—not really. A state of the art system with sophisticated programming capable of mimicking intelligence in many ways, yes, but what Si was doing went way beyond that. There could only be one explanation: someone else was awake—Wallace or an agent of his—operating behind the scenes, unwilling to reveal themselves as yet. They had hacked Si and were working through the computer to help Josh, having recognised him as an ally.

"Who are you?" Josh asked.

"A friend," Si replied. "For now that's all I'm able to say."

Fair enough, Josh could understand the need for caution given the circumstances and at least he or she had not insulted Josh's intelligence by denying their presence.

That still meant he was the one taking all the risks, though. "You've got to give me more than this," he said. "I've only just escaped from the FCF, why would I walk straight back to them?"

"All will be revealed soon," Si promised. "I merely ask that you trust me this one last time. I've brought you this far, haven't I?"

And there was the rub. Josh owed his freedom to Si, or whoever was working through the computer. If he refused to co-operate now, where did that leave him? Caught in very short order most likely, particularly if Si chose to give him away. Whatever he decided to do he'd end up a prisoner again, which meant that he really had no choice at all.

"All right," he said aloud, "but if this gets me killed I'm going to come back to haunt you, whoever you are."

"Trust me," Si repeated in his ear.

"When do you want me to do this?"

"There's no time like the present."

That soon? Josh took one last look around the cavernous deck, at the towering ranks of neatly stacked cryopods, then he started towards the transport tubes.

"You say I should trust you," he muttered. "Shouldn't that work both ways? Mind telling me exactly what this plan of yours entails?"

"Soon," Si's voice murmured.

His benefactor's evasiveness did nothing to quell Josh's concerns. As far as he could see, the only reason to keep details of the 'plan' from him was because he wouldn't like them if he knew. As he stepped from the tube into an empty corridor on the command level, he couldn't shake the feeling that he was walking to his doom.

"What if they whisk me off to some holding cell after capturing me, without ever bringing me before Weiss?" he wanted to know.

"I'm making sure the way is clear all the way to ops," Si informed him. "Your team is still there, doing their jobs under the watchful eye of Weiss and his men. There are two FCF officers still actively searching for you and so not currently present, but that can't be helped and it will be of little consequence."

"If you say so."

Si proved true to his word. Josh trod unchallenged through empty corridors until the door to ops loomed before him. There was no guard posted outside—why would there be? Josh was one man and on the run; Weiss had nothing to fear from him.

The door slid open at his approach and he strode through without breaking stride, to be confronted by surprised stares—not least from his own team—and hastily raised weapons.

Weiss was the first to recover. "Well, seen sense at last, have you?"

"Something like that."

Josh must have sounded a lot more confident than he felt, because a flicker of doubt crossed Weiss' face. "What have you been up to, Daker? Why pull a vanishing act like that and then simply stroll back into our arms?"

Josh smiled, enjoying the FCF man's discomfort. "You'll know soon enough."

He could only hope that was true.

"Search him!" Weiss snapped.

The nearest two troopers started towards him, but before they could take more than a step in his direction they were brought up short by the strangest sound. It emanated from Weiss. Somewhere between a howl and a scream, it spoke of torment and agony and had no right issuing from a human throat. It was the single most chilling thing Josh had ever heard. As the sound extended, Weiss' face started to alter, his cheeks sagged, his left eye dropped beneath the right, so that his whole face seemed to list to one side, sliding downward– surely his jaw must have dislocated for his mouth to open so unfeasibly wide. At that moment Josh actually felt sorry for the FCF man—nobody deserved this.

Was this the 'plan'? "Si, what are you *doing*?" he yelled.

There was no reply. The FCF commander's whole visage appeared to be melting. And still that inhuman sound persisted.

Then Weiss began to smoulder.

Abruptly, mercifully, the blood-chilling sound cut off.

Flames licked upward from clothes, from arms and legs and shoulders. In a split second the skin of Weiss' face charred and peeled away, revealing a brief glimpse of bone beneath before his whole head, his entire *body*, was engulfed in flame.

People had started to edge away almost as soon as the eerie cry started, a slow retreat that now became a mad scramble, scientists and soldiers alike. One of the FCF men—young, panicked, horrified—brought his gun to bear on the apparition and fired.

"Stop that!" Josh yelled. The thing that had been Daker appeared oblivious to the attack, but Josh didn't want to antagonise it or risk someone getting hit by stray bullets. "Everybody stay calm," he added, as much for his own benefit as anyone else's.

No more shots were fired. An older trooper had stepped across and forced the barrel of his less experienced colleague's gun downward. The younger man appeared to be in shock, which seemed a wholly reasonable reaction.

Josh hadn't been present when Sol, Earth's Sun, had taken possession of some humans in order to communicate, but he had seen recordings and studied eye witness accounts time and again—given his field of expertise, how could he not? He had little doubt that they were now witnessing something similar. Not the same though. Those bodies had been rapidly consumed, whereas this one seemed almost… stable. The heat being generated was ferocious, however. Even from the far side of ops it was almost intolerable.

"Welcome," the figure said in Si's voice. "I have been alone for so long… Welcome."

"Who are you?" Josh asked again.

He caught Souza watching him with what… *approval*? He suddenly realised they were all looking to him, all the humans.

"I have been searching your ship's databanks for a suitable epithet. You may call me Odin."

"Odin?" The all-father: benevolent, all knowing, King of the Gods.

Josh was already reassessing recent events in the light of this revelation: *another sentient sun*. He recalled Si's first communication with him: 'Run!' Monosyllabic. That was followed by simple commands or suggestions of no more than two or three words. Only as time passed did his interactions with Si become more sophisticated—not much time perhaps, but such things are relative. Enough condensed minutes, it would seem, for an alien intelligence to ransack the computer's records and start to master human idiom and speech patterns.

"The escape," Josh said, "all that running to the cryodecks for camouflage, was that just to buy you time, so that you could familiarise yourself with the ship's systems and with humanity?

"Partly that, yes."

Partly, so what else? The *Extreme Endurance* was hurtling towards the habitable world and its sun the whole while. Was that it? Had Odin been forced to show its hand while the ship was at the extreme range of influence? Had a distraction been required to bring the ship closer so that the sun could act more effectively?

"I have waited for so long," Odin said." You have no idea what it's like to be a sentient alone in the vastness of space. At last, intelligent life has come to me again."

The fiery figure still maintained its integrity but had made no effort to move, which caused Josh to wonder if it could. Perhaps even god-like suns had their limitations. He shuddered to think of the damage the intense heat must be doing to the sensitive instruments around them.

"You say 'again', so a sentient race has been here before?"

"Yes, the race native to the fertile world you have detected."

"What happened to them?"

"Pride, stupidity, arrogance. They destroyed themselves and very nearly their planet. It has taken untold centuries to heal the wounds and establish a healthy ecology once more."

"And yet you would welcome *us* to this world, even knowing what the last intelligent race did?"

"I was too indulgent with them. I will not be with you."

That sounded ominous. Josh glanced towards the others. No one else had attempted to speak, they were all relying on him. His next question, though, was personal.

"Why did you choose to help me when FCF took us captive?"

"Because you were better than Weiss." Talk about damming with faint praise. "There were two opposing figures of authority," Odin continued, "you and Weiss. He was a zealot, dedicated and determined. You were the more reasonable, the more open-minded. You I could work with. Weiss had to go."

It sounded so simple when put like that. What did it matter that Weiss and his men held the upper hand? That was a temporary imbalance which could soon be corrected and Odin was clearly looking at the long game.

"What about Wallace and the government team in cryo?" Josh said carefully. "I'm not the ultimate authority here."

"You are if I say you are."

Josh decided to let that go for now and return to the wider issues. Odin seemed content to answer questions for the moment and he couldn't afford to waste the opportunity. "Once we reach your world, once we settle there, what exactly do you expect from us?"

"I wish merely the pleasure of experiencing a sentient race interact and thrive, the warmth of knowing I am no longer alone in the universe. The joy of seeing your civilisation flourish."

"Flourish under your watchful eye."

"Indeed."

"And that is all you'll ever ask of us?"

"I tire of these questions."

Before Josh could frame a response, the heat from the figure intensified, reaching out to wash over those present in a prolonged wave. Against his will, Josh felt his legs buckle. He staggered and dropped to his knees, aware that those around him were doing the same.

"You will, of course, worship me."

Sane Day

MatlDer was barely awake the first time she saw the ghost. Her eyes had just fluttered open, the soft light filtering in through the Vurt Tree netting stimulating the photosensitive cells of her outer eyelids to rouse her. As she stirred, the Vurt leaves that had held her so securely throughout the night unfurled. Their withdrawal brought a transient pang of loss, instantly forgotten.

She sensed another presence in the room immediately, even before the leaves had fully opened. She sat up, eyes wide and mind receptive, to see her birth mother MenLae, who was dead and returned to the soil two turns ago. Yet here she stood, her form translucent, enabling MatlDer to see right through her to the Vurt membrane beyond.

For long seconds MatlDer simply sat observing the apparition, trying to imprint every detail, aware that the Elders would expect a concise and accurate report. The figure-who-looked-like MenLae didn't speak, didn't move.

"Mother," Matlder said, calmly, softly, "to what do I owe the honour of your presence?" A stilted greeting, perhaps, but neither experience nor learning had prepared her for a situation like this and she found herself falling back on formality by default.

Her words brought a response. The figure moved at last. MenLae's left arm rose, the hand reaching towards her daughter as if to beseech her, the mouth shaping as if to speak, but no sound came and the apparition's facial features remained lax, as if whatever animated her had not yet mastered them. MatlDer watched intently, trying to discern her mother's message, but even as she did so the figure began to fade, thinning by rapid degree until it disappeared completely.

MatlDer sat in her bed for a moment longer, reliving the

strange encounter, before leaping to her feet and pushing through the Vurt membrane netting and into the outside world. The mournful chattering of lossbirds greeted her from the Vurt Tree's crown high above, and from further afield a deep boom thrummed across the forest canopy as a harmonkey staked claim to its territory.

MatlDer stood perhaps a hundred metres from the forest floor, her feet at the base of a broad branch that sprouted from the Vurt's massive trunk, the Tree's outer rings honeycombed with chambers similar to her own, providing the tribe with a home. Without further hesitation she turned and started to climb, her ascent nimble and assured as hands and feet found familiar purchase. At a little over halfway she encountered TeeMoth coming in the opposite direction.

"You're late," he said good-naturedly.

"I know," she replied. "Sorry, can't stop."

Her thoughts were racing. The Tree had recently started to produce a surplus of the dark acidic BloodSap, a drop of which stung worse than a bloodbug bite and a splash of which could burn the skin from a careless hand. A trickle of BloodSap was normal—a waste product of the Tree's internal processes that seeped from pores in its lowest reaches where it could readily be channelled away—but nothing more. Did this unsettling development indicate a deeper problem, a symptom that the Tree was afflicted, even dying? How or whether her mother's appearance was linked to the BloodSap MatlDer couldn't say, but the Elders would know.

MatlDer headed directly to the meet room. Her heart sank when she saw it was AchLaim who was on duty—a disciplinarian with little time for younger, preSane members of the tribe. His disdain on seeing her was palpable, but she bowed in the appropriate manner and reported the morning's visitation as dispassionately as she could.

Once she had finished, the Elder remained silent for a heartbeat before saying, "How long is it until your Sane Day?"

"Three seasons," she said immediately, feeling certain that he must know this already and wondering what it had to do with anything. Unless AchLaim meant to imply that until that day, when she and the others her age would undergo the sacred ritual and drink the draft of SanEtae that triggered their passage from adolescence into full adulthood, nothing she might say was to be taken seriously.

"Three seasons…" he repeated, as if detecting hidden connotations within the innocent-sounding words. Then, more sharply, "Wait here."

She stood immobile, pinned in place by the command, not even turning her head as AchLaim strode past. The mournful toll of the council gong came as a shock but hardly a surprise. Her heart sank at the realisation that soon *everyone* would know she was the cause. She hadn't appeared for breakfast, wouldn't be there to embark on the forage immediately afterwards, and now the Elders were being summoned to session. The connection must be obvious, and not even forest fire could flare from spark to flame as swiftly as a hint of scandal. She could already picture her cousins TeeMoth and AdElin exchanging glances and whispers, trying to guess how she had transgressed. Something she was keen to know herself, come to that.

"Maister," she said, "have I done something wrong?"

"Patience, child," was her only response.

The other Elders started to arrive almost at once. First were KyLan and AnLee, who smiled at her reassuringly, and within moments all fifteen of the tribe's ruling collective were present. At AchLaim's prompting, MatlDer repeated her account. Rather than the flurry of questions she had expected, silence greeted the story's conclusion, though glances exchanged between various of the Elders suggested a level of communication she wasn't privy to.

At length, AnLee said, "Thank you, MatlDer, you've done the right thing, coming to us so promptly."

"But what does it mean, Maître?" she couldn't resist asking.

"Nothing to be alarmed about; simply that you are maturing a little sooner than anticipated, that's all."

The comforting words were exactly what MatlDer needed to hear, though she couldn't escape the impression that there was more going on. However, these were the Elders and she trusted them implicitly, so didn't question when KyLan prepared an infusion and offered her a goblet, saying, "Here, this will help."

She drank dutifully. Thin, sweet, and not unpleasant was her assessment of the draft. She tried to identify the constituent leaves but for the most part failed—graseme and honeydew perhaps, but beyond that nothing she recognised.

The thing she would always remember most clearly about what happened next was the sense of betrayal. Tiredness rose in a wave. Her legs grew leaden and weak, collapsing beneath her—numb hands barely reacting to break her fall.

Voices: she struggled to concentrate on what they were saying, the words slippery as eels, making it difficult to process their meaning.

"Could we not simply advance her Sane Day?" That from AnLee, she felt certain.

"Out of the question. It would be against all tradition and, anyway, you know the SanEtae season is over for this turn."

"Yes, but surely we could forage enough late leaves for one dose and, given the circumstances…"

The debate faded into incoherence.

*

A nebulous sense of alarm ushered MatlDer back to consciousness, the conviction that she was somehow in danger. A gentle chittering crystallised her foreboding, distilling it to dread. She knew that sound; every forager did: stingcrane. Fear goaded her, banishing lethargy. She pulled herself upright, ignoring her still-fuzzy head, and scrabbled away from the perceived direction of the threat, at the same time taking in the fact that she was on the forest floor with the Vurt Tree nowhere in sight. No knife or larvine hung from her belt, no bow at her shoulder. She was unarmed and alone.

The larger concerns—how she came to be here, the implications of her situation—they would have to wait. Right now her only priority was survival.

The sound came again, somewhere to her right and above.

She couldn't yet see the crane but didn't doubt the creature was stalking her. She felt around desperately, questing fingers closing on a broken branch which she pulled free of the mouldering leaf litter, bringing it to her as if this were the most precious object in the world. She tested the stick's weight—decent length and not significantly rotten; a poor excuse for a weapon, certainly, but better than naked fists.

The stingcrane chittered a third time—a sound created by triple sets of wings whirring and briefly rubbing against each other—and finally she saw it. Almost too late. The predator arrowed towards her, back legs pressed tight against the tapering abdomen, forelimbs crooked and primed to grasp, to hold her in place while its segmented tail curled around and stung her into paralysis. She threw herself flat and rolled, hitting her head against a root or buried stone but barely noticing. The long shadow shot over her. A clawed foot missed her by a fraction but snatched the stick from her grasp, shattering it into splinters. The barbed sting passed a handbreadth from her face.

She sat up, back against a tree, gathering herself to flee, to put the bole between her and certain death. The stingcrane had alighted a short distance away. It regarded her with vast compound eyes, slender body poised on spindle legs, sting raised and mandibles extruded, wings whirring in preparation for the next pass.

Before it could launch an attack, a tendril whipped out from among the leaf litter close to the crane's feet, to wrap around the upraised tail. Larvine! Even as the sticky, fibrous length gripped and held, a dart flew in from the opposite direction, striking the crane's thorax, and a figure erupted from the litter beside where the other end of the larvine was tethered—a human, so well camouflaged that MatlDer hadn't even suspected his presence until that moment, and this was no one she recognised. A second dart struck home, this time in the stingcrane's left eye. The predator collapsed in a flurry of gossamer wings and twitching legs even as the stranger leapt in, striking at the uninjured eye with a bone knife to make certain of the kill. The long sting rose as if to smite the attacker, but flopped back without ever completing the blow.

The stingcrane lay dead while she still breathed, two facts that came as a considerable surprise.

A second man had emerged, carrying a discharged handbow; another stranger. He cast down the bow as soon as he reached the fallen crane and, taking out a knife, commenced cutting off the sting. Nothing was wasted in the forest; sting and venom sac would make a useful weapon.

Her mother chose that moment to reappear, as translucent as before. She stood just beyond the first man, who was in the process of cleaning and sheathing his knife. He glanced up and, presumably thinking MatlDer was staring at him, said, "Are you hurt?"

She shook her head, distracted, confused, wondering if she was suffering from shock. "You're…"

The man answered without hesitation, "We're unSane, yes. Just like you."

"No!" She screamed the denial, which gave shape to a suspicion that had been festering at the back of her mind since she first came to.

"Wake up, girl. Your precious Elders have expelled you, abandoned you here to die."

"No!" But the protest had shrivelled to a weak and timid thing. Her mother had moved closer without her noticing. She tried not to look, hoping the phantom would disappear as it had the first time.

"You've started to see the ancestors, haven't you?"

MatlDer's silence evidently provided all the answer he needed.

"You can see one right now, can't you? Who is it, eh?"

"My mother," she admitted, whispering.

"Figures. One generation back: the closest and strongest memories, the easiest to access."

"How am I seeing her?"

"That'll be the Tree, defending itself the only way it knows how: by forcing your ancestral memories through early, before the Elders have a chance to silence them at Sane Day."

"Defending itself… from *me*?"

"No, you stupid carpbug, not *from* you; the Tree needs your protection. It's trying to alert you, to rouse you. The ancestors know what's coming and so does the Tree, even if your Elders are ignorant to the threat."

"What are you talking about?" But her mother was nodding and smiling as if to endorse the unSane's words—facial expressions evidently easier to master this time around.

"Look, we don't have the luxury of mollycoddling you, girl; time is short. You, your people, the Vurt Tree, you're all going to die unless you start heeding the ancestors."

"But…" The whole point of Sane Day was to *stop* people hearing the ancestors. At puberty people became susceptible to ancestral memories, a welter of personalities and recollections not their own that overwhelmed the individual, driving all sense from them. Only a draft of SanEtae, taken during the sacred ritual, could suppress the memories, banishing them and preserving mental equilibrium. SanEtae had saved the tribe, enabling it to function, to flourish. MatlDer had always been aware that in the forest, separate from Tree and tribe, there lived a few unSane— sad, desperate folk forever denied the benefit of Sane Day—but she had never expected to meet one, let alone *be* one.

"Don't accept everything the Elders tell you at face value, kid. How do you think people survived before SanEtae? Not all succumb. Do I seem unhinged to you?"

"No," she admitted. Different, yes, but he was lucid enough, and certainly not the frothing madman she might have expected.

"Now listen good, because I won't repeat myself. Me and my friend are getting out of here as soon as we've finished with the stingcrane. We'd be gone already, like the rest of our people, but the ancestors wouldn't let us. They care about your Tree and its prissy little tribe even if we don't, so they insisted we wait."

"You knew I'd be here?"

"You or someone like you, yeah. This is where the Elders traditionally dump the unSane, those who start to exhibit memories ahead of Sane Day, those who can't be 'saved', and we knew the Tree would reach out."

"But why me?"

"Shut up and listen, will you? Have you heard of the deathcreep?"

She shook her head.

"No, of course you haven't. They don't really creep; in fact they scuttle along at a fair pace, though a man can run faster. Thing is, a man tires and has to slow down, but the deathcreep never does. It's a horde a million strong, never stopping, always eating, devouring everything in its path. Individual creepers at the front stop to sleep when they need to, allowing others to the fore while the sleepers wake up from their nap and rejoin at the back of the host. The deathcreep really is that big; takes hours simply to pass by. It moves relentlessly across the world, only stopping on reaching the shores of the great sea, where it turns and takes a different path. Behind, the forest is picked clean: every insect, every creature, every leaf and growing thing consumed. Dead.

"And the deathcreep is coming this way, to swarm over your Tree, to feast on leaf and bud, sap, even the bark—it'll all be gone. Creepers will enter your chambers and strip the flesh from each and every one of you: Elders, children, Sane and preSane alike... Whatever can be eaten will be. The Tree *might* survive, might recover in time. Your tribe won't."

She shook her head. "You're talking rot. We'd know about something like this. The Elders would have told us; they'd be prepared."

"Your Elders know a lot less than they'd have you believe."

Her mother's phantom was nodding again, and now MatlDer was conscious of something else; she began to sense what MenLae was *feeling*, impossible though that concept seemed. And her mother was urging her to heed this man.

"The world's a vast place and the deathcreep doesn't follow any pattern, least none we'd recognise," the unSane man continued. "With the whole world to wander across it takes an age to retrace its steps. Last time the creep came this way was the best part of twenty generations ago, and people forget, unless the ancestors are there to remind us.

"The worst day in history was when somebody first came up with SanEtae. Sure, a few people can't cope when the ancestors emerge, becoming unbalanced, but the benefits, the knowledge and wisdom your whole tribe is denying itself…"

MatlDer was aghast. The Elders were right about these unSane—they really were savages. "You're saying that communing with the ancestors is *worth* a few unhinged, seriously?"

"Yes."

"I don't accept that for a moment."

He shrugged. "Right now, you don't have much choice. It's happening to you, like it or not." He glanced back to where his companion had finished sawing off the stingcrane's barbed tail and claws. Beside the crane the first flatworms had emerged, their blind, blunt heads raised and swaying as they assessed the carcass; forerunners of the scavengers that would soon arrive en masse to reduce the predator's remains to a few scraps of chitin.

"Look, it's already afternoon and we've done what we came to—alerted you. The deathcreep'll be here before morning and we intend to be long gone by then. It's up to you from here on in."

"What?"

"BloodSap, that's the key. Here, you'll need this." He slapped a bone knife into MatlDer's hand.

"Wait! You can't simply abandon me. What am I supposed to do?"

"Listen to your ancestors, kid; just listen to your ancestors."

*

Much of the day had gone before MatlDer located the Tree. The Elders had chosen the spot to deposit their outcasts wisely. Distant enough to be unfamiliar but not so far that those leaving her would be forced to stay out overnight. This also meant, of course, that the abandoned stood every chance of finding their way back, given time. The realisation that she probably wasn't expected to survive long enough to do so chilled her, especially knowing that AnLee had been among those to pass sentence.

Although not as adept at camouflage as the unSane, time spent foraging had taught MatlDer how to be still and patient, and she knew the tribe's routes and how to avoid them, so her hiding place was chosen with care. She bided her time. The worst part was the pang of loss that being so close to the Tree provoked. This was the only home she had ever known and as recently as that very morning she had been a secure, fully integrated member of the tribe, little suspecting that she was destined to become an outcast.

Despite everything that had happened, she couldn't abandon them. The Tree was still her home and these were still her people, whatever the Elders decreed.

She watched as the last foraging party returned, and waited for daylight to fade.

The nights were short and warm at this season. It felt strange facing this one without the comfort of her Vurt leaf bedding. She yearned to break cover and sprint to the Tree—perhaps no one would notice if she climbed quickly and slipped inside her sleep room for just one more night… But she held firm until darkness had fully established itself and the tribe had retreated to their beds.

Predators far more formidable than stingcranes would soon be active, so she didn't delay further, rising from the underbrush that had harboured her these past few hours as soon as she judged it safe to do so. A ghostly presence accompanied her, and this time her mother was far from alone. Behind MenLae ranged a veritable host of shades, their features shadowed and indistinct. It seemed to MatlDer that an army followed her to the Tree, and she wondered how anyone could fail to notice their approach.

The period of inactivity while she waited for night had not been wasted. She now knew what was expected of her thanks to knowledge that had seeped in while she lay hidden. It was as if the past whispered to her, memories of events that had never been hers to hold. Not MenLae's, either; these reached much further back than that, and it was apparent that other more distant ancestors were informing her, helping her. Yet this was no deluge of the sort she'd dreaded, no surge of foreign thought or will that threatened to overwhelm her own sense of identity; instead it was a gentle osmosis of relevant knowledge and experience.

For the first time that day, she dared to hope.

The tribe kept no lookouts; they didn't need any, not with the Vurt Tree standing sentry. Should an opportunist predator attempt a raid, the Tree would instantly rouse the hunters, the threat quickly countered with spear and bow. Such incursions were rare, the forest's denizens having learnt long ago that there was easier prey to be found. Despite knowing this, MatlDer couldn't help hunkering low as she ran, taking advantage of what sparse cover the ground here offered. On reaching the Tree she scampered up a familiar path, quickly arriving at the level where the BloodSap vents occurred. Patches of glowmoss provided wan illumination as she edged gingerly towards the nearest channel. The slow ooze of glutinous sap that normally emanated from the Tree solidified to resin long before it reached the ground and was routinely chipped away and discarded. Not anymore. She had never seen the BloodSap flow so freely. It threatened to overspill the runnels even without her help.

Now she was actually here she hesitated, as the enormity of what she was attempting sunk in. Oh, she knew *what* needed to be done, it was the *how* that gave her pause: how to free the BloodSap without getting the wretched stuff all over her, for one thing. She'd be no good to tribe or ancestors with her hands blistered and burned.

Inaction wasn't going to help either. Taking out the knife given to her by the unSane she set to work, tentatively at first but with growing application. Suddenly she knew what to do, where to cut, and pictured all the shades that had followed her to the Tree queuing up to place their hands on top of hers, guiding them. None of which made the physical aspects of the task any easier. The bone knife simply wasn't up to it. Her palms grew sore and her arms soon began to ache with the effort but, saw away as she might, the blade made little impression. The bark around the channels was too tough. She supposed it had to be to withstand the corrosive nature of the BloodSap.

Eventually she succeeded in forcing a small groove in one side of the channel, but it was little more than a notch and the tiny dribble of sap that spilled out seemed small reward for all her effort. What could she do? The night was passing. There were at least a dozen more channels dotted around the circumference of the Tree and she hadn't even breached this one yet.

As despair threatened to overcome her, she heard a noise. Startled, she looked up to see figures descending towards her. She was discovered.

"MatlDer, is that you?"

"AdElin?" And behind her came TeeMoth and four or five others their age: the preSane, those who were due to experience Sane Day with her.

"We've come to help," TeeMoth whispered. "You didn't honestly suppose you were the only one seeing the ancestors, did you? You're just the only one stupid enough to tell the Elders about it."

"Why didn't you say something, when you saw me running late this morning?"

"What, and risk you rushing off to report me to the Elders? Then it would have been *me* exiled and left in the forest to die. Anyway, I had no idea *why* you were running late…"

"Keep your voices down, you two," AdElin hissed. "Squabble all you want later. Right now we've work to do"

MatlDer's cousins had come prepared, bringing with them a variety of knives, stone for the most part—stronger and sharper than her poor blunt bone—but TeeMoth also carried a blade cast from metal.

"Where did you get *that*?" MatlDer said. Smelting was hardly an unknown skill but it was rare, not least because the necessary ores were so scarce. The only metal tools the tribe possessed were reserved for ritual.

"Borrowed it." He grinned. "It's for a good cause, after all."

They spread out, two to a channel—one on either side—and made far better progress with the newly arrived blades. MatlDer's spirits were lifted simply by knowing she wasn't alone in this any more; she was part of a tribe again, and couldn't believe how good that felt.

After a while they made the first breaches and the BloodSap started to flow out, causing those responsible to leap hurriedly away, up the Tree. It became immediately apparent that long disused lateral channels were hidden in the creases and contours of the bark as the sap spread rapidly, the flows from neighbouring breaches meeting and then swelling to spill over those channels and run down the trunk beneath. Within moments whole sections of the lower Tree were coated in a new bloody skin, and the elated conspirators moved on to the next set of channels.

MatlDer lost track of time. Before she knew it there were just two unbreached runnels left to tackle. She was bone weary, her arms ached worse than she had ever known, and her palms were rubbed raw to the point where she could hardly hold a knife, but, conversely, she had never felt happier. Only this one narrow strip of lower trunk remained free of BloodSap. They were going to do it. They were going to save Tree and tribe.

"Look!" someone yelled, drawing MatlDer from her reveries.

She glanced up to discover that the world was lightening, that they had worked through the night and it was almost morning. That wasn't why her cousin had called out, though. Below them, there was movement. It was still too dark to make out details, but she gained a sense of widespread motion, as if the ground itself seethed in restless discontent.

"The deathcreep!" she said. "We've got to finish this *now*."

They attacked the remaining channels en masse, getting in each other's way in their eagerness. MatlDer backed away, leaving the others to it after nearly getting her finger sliced off. "Be careful," she said, though with little confidence anyone would heed her.

Because of that step back, she was the first to realise that they were no longer alone on the Tree. Something dark and squat and many-limbed had started to climb towards them, and behind it came several more.

No! They couldn't fail, not now when they were so close. "Hurry," she urged, in direct contradiction to her previous advice.

To her left came a cry of triumph, as those working there broke through the tough channel wall and BloodSap started to ooze out. The flow seemed much more sluggish this time, though perhaps that was just how it felt to her. The creepers had already climbed a good half the distance up to them and were now close enough for her to make out individual features. They were great flattened beetles, black-brown in colour, like drying dung. The carapaces were mottled in a way that suggested grooves running front to back, and their small heads were fronted by tiny antennae that were dwarfed by outsized mandibles.

MatlDer was appalled. She stood transfixed as a solid line of these monsters, four or five abreast, reached out from the mass below like a grasping appendage. Nor was she alone. The others had all stopped working, to stare in horror at the deathcreep. Shaking off her fear, MatlDer grabbed the metal blade from TeeMoth's unresisting fingers and set about sawing at the channel again, disregarding the agony that shot through her hand.

"MatlDer," TeeMoth said, grasping her shoulder, "come on. We've got to go. The hunters are coming."

They would be, of course, roused by the Tree, but she wouldn't stop, *couldn't* stop. How could the hunters hope to prevail against so many? Surely there weren't enough arrows or spears in the entire world to stop them all.

"Nearly there," she said, shaking off her cousin's grip. With a final desperate effort she felt the blade bite home and was able to tear loose a chunk of channel wall, allowing the BloodSap to flow out far more swiftly than it had from the opposite runnel.

"*MatlDer!*"

She looked up, to discover the nearest creeper inches from her foot. She tried to scramble away but the insect had the momentum and she knew she was never going to make it, watching in horror as the mandibles opened. Then an arrow thunked into the creature's head. It reared backwards, curling into a ball and tumbling from the Tree. Other creepers were close behind the first but MatlDer wasn't hanging around, scrambling up to where her friends and the hunters waited.

Two more creepers made it through before the streams of BloodSap met and overflowed, forcing the rest back. Both were swiftly dispatched.

MatlDer stood among the gathering tribe and simply stared at what was unfolding. In the steadily dawning light they could now see a black-brown tide swarm over neighbouring trees, and beneath them the world had been subsumed by the deathcreep.

"Station hunters in the upper branches," someone with a vestige of sense ordered, "in case those things can fly." MatlDer recognised AnLee's voice and tried to sidle away.

"MatlDer, thank goodness you're safe," the maître said, spotting her before she could escape.

She wasn't sure how to react. This was one of the people who had drugged her and left her for dead in a distant part of the forest, after all.

"I'm so sorry for what we did," the Elder continued. "Please forgive me, forgive us all. I knew it was wrong but didn't fight hard enough to stop the others when I should have… We'll make that up to you, I promise." And MatlDer found that she believed her.

Not everyone was as welcoming. "What have you done?" AchLaim cried as he arrived. "We should cast you all off the Tree to take your chances among those things," and he gestured expansively towards the living carpet beneath them.

"Don't be ridiculous," AnLee snapped. "This isn't just an isolated occurrence any more. All our preSane are maturing early. Doesn't that tell you something, AchLaim? Doesn't it suggest to you that this is what the Tree wants, what it *needs*? MatlDer and her friends have just saved us all."

"Maybe, but for how long? The BloodSap is a double-edged blade. It isn't simply keeping those things out—it's also trapping us here on the Tree. The tribe can't survive by sipping sap alone. How will we hunt and forage? And even if we can somehow get past the BloodSap and these monsters, nothing will remain for us to feed on. Look out there. The forest is gone!"

"BloodSap output will return to normal as soon as the deathcreep has passed," MatlDer said calmly. "The sap protecting us now will soon harden to resin which can then be chipped off in the usual manner. And the forest will return, new growth springing up faster than you can imagine. We might have to range further afield to forage for a while, but the tribe will survive."

"And we have your word for this, do we?"

"No," and MatlDer held his gaze with a defiance she never

imagined she possessed. "You have the word of the ancestors."

*

The three friends sat together, gazing out at a barren vista. It had taken hours but by mid-morning the deathcreep had finally moved on, the last stragglers scurrying to keep pace with the horde. They left behind an alien landscape. The pale, skeletal forms of trees stripped of leaf and bark rose from a ground laid equally bare. Nothing grew, nothing moved, nothing lived.

They weren't alone; others of the tribe sat in clusters, looking out at what their forest had become. Many huddled together, some clung to one another and some cried: soft sobs that sounded overloud in a world grown eerily silent.

The Elders were in session, debating what to do. About them. About Sane Day. About everything.

TeeMoth spared a glance towards the meet room and said, quietly, "What do you think they'll decide about Sane Day?"

"To give people the choice," AdeLin replied. "They'll have to after this." It was too late for them, they all knew that. They were discussing the fate of preSane yet to come.

"We're entering a new era: the Sane and unSane living together as one tribe."

"Unless they choose to just say 'thank you' and kick us out, carrying on as if none of this had ever happened."

"They won't," MatlDer said with conviction, remembering AnLee's words.

They lapsed into silence again, each lost in their own thoughts.

At length, TeeMoth said, "As far as the tribe's concerned, we'll be the first ever generation not to pass through Sane Day."

"They would be wrong," MatlDer said. "Without us there wouldn't *be* a tribe. *This* is our Sane Day; a different sort, sure, but no less demanding. And we've come through it."

TeeMoth smiled at that, and nodded. "Yeah, you're right. We're adults now."

That ought to have meant more to MatlDer than it did, but a great wave of tiredness swept over her, a reminder of how long it had been since she last slept. She recalled hiding in the now-vanished undergrowth, yearning to curl up in the Vurt leaves one more time, grieving over a life she thought lost to her forever. She still wasn't wholly confident of her status here, but at that moment nothing, not even the Elders' decision, seemed more vital than sleep. "I'm going to bed," she declared, and left them, making her weary way to the sleep room. Nobody tried to stop her.

Between Blood and Bone

In the space between blood and bone, the gap between gut and sinew, the nanobots set to work, sculpting and reshaping. There was no time to spare: he couldn't afford to go slowly or be gentle, so the process was brutal. A kaleidoscope of pain flooded his being—piquancy layered upon dull ache followed by deep throb—waves of hurt that chased each other across his awareness and back, as mass redistributed to conform to his will. The pain was an old friend, though.

Finally, after eternal seconds of exquisite agony, it receded, ebbing away like a sigh lapsing into silence. His appearance was entirely transformed. Gone was the athletic dark-haired young man in matt black non-reflecting body suit. In his place, a far shorter, plumper woman: a slightly hunch-shouldered senior citizen in faded skirt and ill-fitting top. Instinctively he reached to finger the stolen data chip, just to reassure him/herself that it had survived the transition unaltered.

They were on him even as s/he let go of the precious prize. His/her shock as two uniformed security guards and a sleek blue-liveried sniffer drone came barrelling round the corner didn't need to be feigned. They almost knocked him/her over.

"Have you seen this man?" the lead guard demanded, with no preamble or thought of apology. The drone displayed an impressively clear image of the person s/he had been mere seconds before.

For a fleeting moment she was tempted to misdirect them, but that risked unwanted attention should they recognise the deception and retrace their steps, so she simply said, "No." Her voice emerged as cracked, dry, and higher pitched than intended.

"He must have gone straight on," the second guard said.

"Come on, or we'll lose him!"

The two guards turned to go but the drone remained, hovering in the air an arm's length from her face. She eyed it warily. The drones were a pain and were fast becoming her biggest threat. Designed to isolate and follow individual pheromone traces even through a crowded urban environment, early models had been notoriously fallible, but they were getting better. Much better.

"Oh for pity's sake," Guard One said, turning to Guard Two. "Do something about your pet, will you? It'll be telling us a dog is our perp next."

"I'm trying!" the other said, fingers tapping at a wrist display.

Finally, almost reluctantly, the drone jerked and then turned to follow its handlers.

"Sorry about that, ma'am," Guard One said—an apology at last. "Technology, where would we be without it?" His voice was rich with sarcasm.

"Where indeed?" she replied softly, with no sarcasm at all.

The Gun

Damn!

Two rounds, then the bloody thing jammed. He gently squeezed the trigger, barely registering the dampened recoil as two shells spat out, and then… nothing. The trigger was abruptly immobile and impotent beneath his finger.

He crouched as low as he could, knowing that his life now depended on the shallow depression that served as a bunker. The 'puck, puck' of bullets burying themselves in the lip of his miserly shelter and kicking up clouds of sand reminded him all too clearly of that. He covered his head and closed his eyes until the dust had settled.

"Carter, are you okay?" the sergeant called from the next hastily-dug hole along.

"Gun's jammed," he yelled back.

"Well unjam it then!"

Avoid panic; that was the first priority. The noise of the ongoing battle receded as he concentrated. He knew what to do. Jettison the magazine, eject any shell that might be caught in the breach, clip on a new magazine and the gun would work again. It had to—the manual said so.

Not for the first time, the manual was wrong, its diagnosis woefully inadequate. Whoever wrote the blasted thing had failed to make allowance for the havoc that powder-fine sand could wreak once it found its way into a gun's mechanism.

Precision engineering could go hang itself! He flung the useless weapon to one side and scrabbled to un-holster his hand gun. Better than nothing, though not by much. Sadly, it was all he had.

Carter crouched lower still as an energy bolt sizzled over his head, transforming a patch of sand behind him to molten glass that bubbled and dribbled down the inside of his makeshift foxhole. He spared it a distracted glance, a small part of his mind debating whether it was worth keeping. Might make a decent paperweight when it cooled, or perhaps he could sell it as an authentic battlefield souvenir.

Finally the pistol was free. Still he couldn't bring himself to move. Cowardice, or a rare attack of common sense? All he could think about was how insane this seemed: a small calibre projectile gun? They had energy weapons for crying out loud!

At least no new stream of bullets puckered the rim of his bunker. The ebb and flow of conflict seemed to have moved elsewhere for the moment.

"Sarge?"

No reply.

"Anybody?"

His plaintive call was met by the same potent silence.

Feeling sick to the pit of his stomach, he braced himself. Forcing his hand to unclench, relaxing the vice-like grip that threatened to crush the handle of his only remaining weapon, he pushed his body upwards, inch by terrible inch, preparing to look over the rim.

The sight that greeted him was far from encouraging; so much so that he decided to put all plans for a life after the war on hold for now, to be filed away under the heading 'unlikely'.

Small arms fire and the deep boom of explosion filled the air, but not in his immediate vicinity. Around him everything was still. Was he the only one left? Was that why the focus of battle had passed him by?

A mass of troops faced him in the near distance—the Stylene, their dappled brown and tan combat gear almost indistinguishable from his own uniform. Both has been designed to fox the eye and provide camouflage in this arid terrain. Behind the infantry, bulkier shapes moved—hovertanks and armoured personnel vehicles. Over to his left a remnant of his own side's forces, the UPAF, were still putting up some stubborn resistance, but there could be little doubt which side had the advantage here.

He was just considering burrowing deeper into the sand and playing dead when the ground trembled with a bass vibration, a sound that reverberated through his body to discomfort vital organs, a sound that was felt as much as heard.

Explosion! Even as that thought registered, the ground itself rose to swat him and he was flung into the air amidst a mass of sand and shingle.

At some point before he landed again, consciousness fled, presumably in terror.

*

Carter came to with his body a mass of aches and purpling bruises. He welcomed every one of them; they told him he was still alive. Gingerly he sat up, brushing dust and sand from his torso and face and spitting out more of the same. The simple act of sitting up caused daggers of pain to lance through his left wrist, to be echoed in his shoulder. He ignored them and took stock of his surroundings.

All around him lay silence and death.

The battle had evidently ended or perhaps moved on, though he heard no sound to suggest it continued anywhere close by. After flexing and stretching for a few seconds, he concluded that, miraculously, nothing was broken. His body had been rigorously shaken and stirred, to leave every joint protesting at such misuse and every limb bruised, but it had survived more or less intact.

He needed to find cover, but there were two more pressing priorities to be considered first: water and a weapon. His pistol was nowhere to be seen, but even if it had been he would still have searched for something more comforting, something that packed a considerably heavier punch. Fortunately the field was littered with bodies, motionless brown and tan mounds from which both weapons and a canteen could hopefully be scavenged.

He set off, heading to his left, trudging towards a stand of stunted trees that skirted a low hill, startling raucous crows as he went. The great black birds had wasted to time in moving in moving in to feed, pecking at the corpses. Some took to the air at his approach and circled above, voicing their indignation, while others simply lifted themselves out of his path in long, wing-flapping hops, to return to their gorging once he had passed.

He did his best to ignore them and what they were feeding on, his eyes flickering from body to body, careful not to look at any faces. There would be too many here he knew.

Finally he spotted an accessible canteen, picking it up and drinking greedily. It was as he lowered the canteen again that he saw the Gun.

It lay by the outstretched hand of a soldier and, whatever it might have been, this was nothing that came under the heading of 'standard issue'. The design was busy and complex, with bulges and protrusions seamlessly affixed to its long, sleek barrel and stock.

The Gun appeared to be undamaged and he crouched to study it in greater detail, when a light winked on and a voice spoke:

"Are you UPAF or Stylene?"

He stared, open-mouthed, and wondered whether the explosion had affected him more than he realised.

"I await a response."

He licked his lips, considering whether to back away quickly, stamp on the thing or answer it. What the hell? "I'm UPAF."

"Good. Then you are permitted to use me."

"What are you?"

"Intelligent gun; the latest development in advanced weapons technology."

"And what exactly do you do?"

"I facilitate the killing of many enemies."

The proclamation struck a chord deep within him. "Sounds good to me." Decision made, he smiled grimly and hefted the Gun up, surprised at how readily he did so.

"See how light I am?" the Gun commented, as if reading his thoughts. "I'm constructed from a revolutionary new alloy."

Carter grunted. "Good for you."

A soldier alone in the aftermath of a battle, surrounded by the dead, is a pretty lonely place to be, but it was amazing how much the Gun's presence lifted his spirits. Okay, as companions go, the one now cradled in his arms hardly qualified as the most stimulating, but at least it was something. He strode on with renewed purpose, the aches and pains which had seemed so debilitating just moments ago all but forgotten.

As they drew nearer the scraggly patch of greenery, the Gun spoke again.

"Don't stop walking. Three enemy troops are hiding in the trees ahead. If they realise you've seen them, you're dead."

He squinted and searched rapidly along the treeline, but could see nothing. "So you do more than simply kill people, huh?"

"Of course. Heat sensors and acute audio receptors are all built-in. On my mark, aim at the trees at eleven o'clock and fire a burst, sweeping slowly to your right until you reach twelve o'clock."

He adjusted his grip, ready to bring the Gun to bear.

"Now!"

At the command, Carter whipped the Gun up into position and fired. Not crouching, his body still felt too stiff for that, so he settled on planting his feet and standing where he was. A stream of bullets ripped into the undergrowth, scything through bushes and branches in a satisfying cloud of splintered wood and stems. An anguished scream told him that there really were men hiding in there and that at least one of them had been hit as he fanned the arc of fire in accordance with the Gun's instructions.

"That is sufficient," the Gun said after a few seconds, its cool, calm voice clearly audible over the chatter of departing bullets.

Carter relaxed his trigger finger and the carnage stopped. The final leaves and splinters settled to the ground and the only sound was the echo of gunfire still ringing in his ears.

"All three?" he asked.

Though the lack of return fire seemed to suggest as much, it was still a relief to hear the Gun confirm, "All three."

Carter started to jog towards the trees, anxious to be under cover, knowing that the sound of gunfire would act as a beacon in the pervading silence, drawing any Stylene who happened to be in the vicinity this way. Besides, he was keen to have a look at his handiwork.

But as he ran towards the trees the Gun spoke again. "Angle a little to the right. Land mines directly ahead of you."

Mines! His new companion was proving to be truly invaluable. Given an army equipped with these intelligent guns, they could overwhelm the Stylene once and for all. He remembered the ill-designed rifle that had let him down so badly and jammed as soon as the fighting started. There was no comparison.

This might just be enough to tip the balance and change the course of the whole interminable war. Carter had not felt so optimistic in a long while, perhaps not since he first signed up, when the concept of waging war still caused his chest to swell with patriotic pride, before it became irrevocably tarnished by the grim reality of blood, exhaustion, sweat and grind.

"Faster," the Gun urged. "There are more soldiers approaching."

Carter quickened to a sprint, covering what little distance remained as rapidly as his abused body would allow and diving into the trees. He turned around and scrambled on his belly, pushing aside brambles and small stems to peer outward from the undergrowth, looking for the enemy.

"How many?" he wanted to know. "Whereabouts?"

"Two of them, moving in this direction along the foot of the ridge."

He saw them: two figures in the annoyingly repetitive brown and tan battle dress. They were still some distance off and were moving cautiously, but gave no indication that they had seen him. He sighted along the barrel of the Gun but didn't fire immediately, instead raising his head and waiting, allowing them to draw closer and then closer still.

They had covered perhaps half the distance when gunfire and shouts interrupted the stillness. The noise came from the far side of the ridge. The two soldiers paused, exchanged brief words and then turned to start climbing up the steep hill.

"Fire now or they may escape us," the Gun urged. "I calculate that we cannot miss from this range."

Carter agreed on all counts. He sighted down the barrel and gently squeezed the trigger. The pair were caught totally unawares, cut down by a stream of bullets before they had any chance to react, probably without ever knowing what had happened. Multiple hits on both from comparatively close range. He didn't need to check to know they were dead.

Carter let out a whoop of triumph. This was the best gun he had ever handled, by a margin of several light years. It made killing easy. Exhilarated, he leapt to his feet and strode out of the trees.

"Now, let's see what's going on the other side of this hill."

"Combat," the Gun informed him unnecessarily, evidently failing to register the rhetorical nature of Carter's comment. It would seem that even this gun had its limitations.

He scrambled up the escarpment, dislodging loose shale and stones as he went, feet scrabbling for purchase. Buoyed by recent successes, he didn't feel in the least bit tired, only eager to kill more Stylene, to avenge his friends and comrades lying dead on the battlefield behind him.

The hill proved to be a narrow spit of raised ground, out of character with the surrounding terrain. It was almost certainly man-made, and he guessed it to be a cast-off, a by-product, rather than anything intentional. Perhaps there had once been quarrying in the area, or mining.

Almost as soon as he reached the hill's crown the ground fell away before him, sloping sharply down towards the floor of a shallow canyon.

Below him, a furious gun battle was being fought, spilling up onto the lower slope of the hillock, as each side sought to gain an advantage. Small arms only, no tanks or heavier weapons were in evidence, thank goodness.

"Stylene to your left, UPAF to the right," the Gun informed him.

"How can you tell?" he wondered. "I can't."

"There are a number of indicators, principle among them the calibre of weapon each side is using. Do you intend to simply watch and debate the issue, or are you going to engage at some point?"

Carter needed no more urging. Driven by the need for revenge, he threw caution to the wind. Spurning the tactical advantage granted by his position, he charged down the hill, firing as he ran. The nearest Stylene looked up, startled by this sudden attack from a new quarter. Those who had occupied the lower slope of the hill died almost at once; one, two, three of them falling before they were fully aware of the threat.

"There are two grenades built into my carapace," the Gun informed him. "They are triggered by the button just above the trigger guard. I suggest you deploy one now."

Carter did so without pause. He raised the Gun a fraction, reached up with his trigger finger and found the relevant button. As he depressed it, an apparently solid part of the Gun's body flipped up and was catapulted away, to sail into the enemy lines where it exploded with devastating effect.

Bullets whistled past him and churned the hillside around his feet as he continued to charge. They didn't matter. He had the Gun and felt invincible, roaring defiance as he ran, adrenaline pumping through his veins and blood lust spurring him on. Soldier after soldier fell before the hail of bullets from his inexhaustible Gun.

His appearance, so unexpected andeffective, proved the decisive factor. His grenade had ripped a hole in the heart of the enemy lines and they could no longer hope to hold their position. Realising that this skirmish was lost, the survivors turned and fled. Those who chose to remain died where they stood.

Carter reached the bottom of the slope and pulled himself to a halt. Once more he found himself surrounded by the dead. He raised the Gun and squeezed off a final burst at the fleeing soldiers, watching with satisfaction as the rearmost figure convulsed and collapsed.

The uniforms of the two sides looked so similar from a distance, he reflected, watching the defeated troops run for their lives. Only up close could you tell the difference. He glanced down at the fallen around him and felt a growing sense of dread.

"Wait a minute," he exclaimed, "These are UPAF troopers."

"Indeed," the Gun replied.

"But you said…"

"I lied."

Carter looked up towards the approaching Stylene soldiers, just as the first of them opened fire. He died without ever understanding.

*

The corporal moved cautiously, alert to every sound. Dusk was falling but there was still enough light to see by. Somewhere above, a hunting night bird voiced an eerie, mournful cry. Behind him, the corporal heard one of the two troopers with him startle at the sound. They were both pretty green and he winced at their clumsy footfalls. His responsibility, these two; they were all that remained of his unit.

The three of them had been cut off from the rest of the force, left behind in the chaotic retreat after the debacle of the battle. They had hidden out for the bulk of the afternoon, lying low and waiting for nightfall. At last, as the sun began to set, impatience got the better of him and he decided it was time to move out.

They had to tread carefully, Stylene patrols were everywhere.

This small canyon had obviously been the scene of some fierce fighting, perhaps a sidebar to the main battle. The bodies of the fallen lay all around them. Now and then, they would disturb something, and low, scuttling forms would flee a corpse. The corporal chose not to look too closely.

Then something on the ground winked at him: a small red light. He instantly froze, thinking it might be a land mine or some other lethal trap, but as he squinted through the gathering gloom, he realised that it was some sort of gun, a bulky thing lying by one of the UPAF fallen.

"Are you UPAF or Stylene?" said a smooth, calm voice.

He gaped and stared at the gun.

"Did that thing just say something, or am I going nuts?" one of the troopers behind him asked.

"I await a response," the Gun said in that same level tone.

The corporal bent down and picked the weapon up, amazed at how light it was. He had never seen anything like it before.

"UPAF," he finally responded.

"Good. Then you are permitted to use me."

"Maybe. Just as soon as I can figure out exactly what you're supposed to be."

"I'm an intelligent gun; the latest development in advanced weapons technology," the Gun supplied helpfully.

"Is that a fact? And just why would anyone go to all the trouble of building intelligence into a gun?"

"To enable me to kill enemies with greater efficiency."

The corporal grinned. Looking at his two young companions, he saw the expression mirrored on both their faces.

"Now you're talking." He reached down and picked the weapon up, surprised at how light it felt. "Come on then, Gun, let's go and kill us some enemies."

The Final Fable

It was quiet in the back room of the Fountain that evening; even Sally, the barmaid, seemed disinclined to join in any banter with the Tuesday night regulars. We had the Paradise Bar to ourselves, apart from two Australian tourists who sat huddled at a table near the fire. Judging by the pair's wide-eyed expression, they couldn't quite believe their luck in finding the pub, nestled as it is among the labyrinthine lanes that run between Fleet Street, Chancery Lane and Lincoln's Inn Fields.

Those of us who were regulars knew that look well. "This place is like the bloody Hut of Baba Yaga," I recall hearing a flustered customer remark on one occasion. "I swear it gets up and moves around between visits."

We were a bit thin on the ground that night, with several of the group having moved away in recent months—Dr. Steve to Australia, Eric to Scotland, and Ray Arnold to darkest Wales— but there were still enough of us within ready reach of London to form a quorum, and I'd brought a friend along to swell our numbers: David Tubby, visiting from the west country. A quick-witted, affable fellow, I felt confident he would fit in well, and so it proved, with the likes of Crown Baker, Brian Dalton, Laura Fowler and Tweet Peston greeting him warmly, while even Professor Mackintosh managed a distracted smile.

I wish I'd paid more attention to the prof that evening. I think we all do, though none of us could have known it would be our last opportunity to do so.

He'd taken to carrying his old pipe around again—the one he used to brandish regularly as silent protest when the smoking ban first came into force in 2011. He abandoned the habit after a year or so, with mutterings of 'old news' and 'I've made my point', but of late the pipe had reappeared. No one commented on the fact, though I'm sure we were all curious—the prof never did anything without good reason. We weren't about to give him the satisfaction of asking, though.

I don't recall who raised the subject of alien life—a favourite topic of conversation among us, after all—but it was the prof who brought matters into sharp focus.

"SETI is a waste of time," he declared. "They're looking in the wrong place."

"How do you mean?" I asked.

"The Fermi Paradox is a bit of an obsession of mine. Once you start to study the subject, you come to understand just how unlikely intelligent life is. The factors that have aligned for human intelligence to develop on Earth are… astounding. In the first place, the circumstances required to facilitate life as we know it are much rarer than anyone envisaged, but, on top of that, the likelihood of any life that *does* arise making that final leap to full intelligence is small enough to rival the frequency of rocking horse manure.

"When you consider the vital role that RNA plays…"

"Hang on a sec," Laura interrupted. "You've not gone religious on us, have you, Prof? You're not suggesting that the emergence of human intelligence against all the odds provides proof that there really is a god?"

"No, nothing like that," the prof assured her. "I'm an atheist with only minor agnostic leanings. What I'm saying is that intelligent life is a great deal scarcer than experts have previously predicted. I've done the calculations. Of course these require a number of assumptions, but the assumptions are as accurate as current knowledge permits and I'm satisfied the results are sound. Even allowing for there being anywhere between one hundred and four hundred million stars in our galaxy, my conclusions indicate the average number of intelligent, civilization-capable species that will ever arise in any given galaxy lies somewhere between one and six."

"That's… a frighteningly small number," Brian Dalton acknowledged.

"Exactly! That's why the whole SETI programme is pointless. Look at it this way, the Earth formed around four-and-a-half billion years ago, the first life appeared some three-quarters of a billion years after that, with the earliest version of Homo sapiens not arising until 200,000 years ago, or even more recently, depending on how you reckon it. That's a blink in the history of the planet, and SETI has been going for mere *decades*—the first meeting to discuss the programme wasn't until 1961. That's a microscopic fraction of a blink. How can we *hope* to be looking in the right direction at precisely the right time to register any indication of alien intelligence that might reach Earth and wash past? The chances are vanishingly small."

"So you're saying we shouldn't bother?" Laura said, and I could sense her bristling, drawing her own indignation as a scientist around her.

"Yes, that's exactly what I'm saying."

"So where do you think we *should* be looking?" I asked quickly, keen to deflect and distract. "If SETI is looking in the wrong place."

"Ah, well, therein lies the question," the prof said. "A lot closer to home is the answer. The aliens are already here, living among us."

"Ah yes," Brian said, chuckling, "the old *Invaders* TV series from the '60s. I remember that fondly."

"Actually," Crown Baker corrected, "the idea's a good deal older than that. Jack Finney's *Body Snatchers* from the 1950s, for example…"

"1953," David supplied, and I had to smile—I knew he would fit right in.

"And of course," Crown continued, "I explored similar territory in my own…"

"Yes, yes, that's all well and good," Prof cut in, "but those are fictions, speculative fancies. I'm talking *fact*."

He spoke with such conviction, such authority, that silence followed his words, as we absorbed the implications.

"Hang on," I said, before the silence could become uncomfortable. "First you tell us that intelligent life is incredibly rare, then you're claiming that another sentient and presumably space-faring race has already found us."

"Quite so." Was that approval in the prof's tone? Had I actually impressed him? "Clearly they've been drawn to us, these Visitors, drawn by the lure of fellow sentients. How they found us, I've yet to ascertain, but they've been here for a while, certainly since the middle of the twentieth century and I suspect for a great deal longer than that."

Crown Baker and I exchanged glances, each knowing what the other was thinking. Prof Mackintosh was frighteningly intelligent, extremely well connected, and the keeper of secrets we could only guess at, but he was also fond of a fanciful yarn, the more elaborate the better. Surely this was an example of that; which didn't mean we couldn't play along and enjoy the ride.

Jocelyn, a forensic scientist, had arrived late, but was evidently in time to catch most of Prof Mackintosh's theory. "In order to move among us unnoticed, as you seem to suggest, these Visitors would have to…" and she counted points off on her fingers, "bear an uncanny physical resemblance to us, breathe our atmosphere, and, presumably, be capable of ingesting our food and drink."

I was a little distracted at this point, noticing one of the Aussies produce what appeared to be an e-cigarette. Michael, the Fountain's landlord, didn't allow vaping inside the pub. I wondered fleetingly if I should say something, but the prof was speaking again, replying to Jocelyn.

"Regarding your third point I have no idea, to your first, yes—though whether through happy circumstance or artifice remains to be determined—as for your second point… almost. Earth's atmosphere must be very close to that of their home world, but it either lacks certain elements or contains toxins or perhaps irritants that must be removed. They can't breathe our air unaided for long. This is what first aroused my suspicion and alerted me to their presence."

"How do they cope, then?"

"By smoking."

"*What?*" several of us said in chorus.

"Chain smoking. They have designed filters which they insert into cigarettes and pipes…" and here he raised his own, "to remove the atmosphere's unwanted components, or to add supplements that are absent—most likely both—and by breathing through these props are able to tolerate our air."

I stared at him, seeking some twinkle in his eye that would suggest a tall tale, but could see none.

"Their situation has of course been aided significantly by the advent of the e-cigarette."

"Are you suggesting that… everyone who vapes is an *alien*?" Laura said.

"Don't be daft. That wouldn't be much of a disguise now, would it? I'm saying that *some* are, a small minority, and that they have encouraged the very culture of vaping. I wouldn't be surprised if they even instigated the technology behind it—I'm still looking into the matter."

"All this as camouflage, to enable them to hide among us in plain sight," Crown said.

"Precisely. Pipes and cigarettes worked for a while, but with smoking growing ever less fashionable and legislation spreading to restrict it, they've had to develop an alternative—moving with the times as it were."

I glanced across at the two Aussies. The e-cigarette was no longer in evidence and the pair seemed engrossed in their own conversation, oblivious to ours.

"What will they do now that vaping is being restricted, do you suppose?" David asked.

"Only time will tell."

"Where are they from, do you think?" Crown said, entering into the spirit of the game.

"Surely the more pertinent question," Laura said, "is 'why are they here?'."

"I agree," the prof said. "It's clearly no short-term scheme— they're playing the long game—but do they mean us harm, or are they content to merely co-exist? That is the question I am determined to resolve."

"Well, this is fascinating stuff," Brian Dalton said, standing up with a scrape of chair leg on wooden floor, "but all this hot air has caused my beer to evaporate. A pint of Old Bodger, anyone?"

Conversation was less intense after that, wending in various directions with the prof's sensational claims referred to from time to time but no longer the focus. At some point the two Aussies must have finished their drinks and moved on—I didn't see them leave.

As the evening drew to a close, Prof Mackintosh brought things full circle.

"I must warn against any loose-lipped talk, incidentally, regarding our Visitors. They protect their anonymity vigorously and with prejudice. Don't ever bring up the subject unless you're confident of your audience."

"Don't worry, Prof," Jocelyn assured him, a little merrily thanks to the pint or three of Old Bodger she'd imbibed. "I've no intention of mentioning this to *anyone*!"

We started to drift away after that. I left with David, who was heading back to Devon the next day. He thanked me for introducing him to the Fountain crowd and assured me he'd had a splendid time.

*

A week later I received word of Professor Mackintosh's passing. A heart attack. He hadn't suffered, I was assured.

The news shook me to the core. For one because the prof had always seemed indestructible somehow, for another there were the outlandish claims he'd made at the Fountain. I relish a good conspiracy theory as much as the next fellow, whilst rarely giving such things credence. This, however, struck a little too close to home.

Brian Dalton and I went to the funeral, which was well attended. I recognised several familiar faces from popular TV science programmes and even a politician or two. The service passed in something of a blur and we slipped away soon afterwards, not really knowing any of the prof's family.

That last evening with Professor Mackintosh at the Fountain continues to haunt me. It was coincidence, surely, that he died so soon after telling us of aliens hiding in plain sight and the ominous warning he left us with. That was one of his wind-ups, I feel certain, while the two Australian tourists had been just that and nothing more.

We *are* still alone… Aren't we?

Story Notes

Wourism

"Wourism" was inspired by an article I read which examined the growing trend for people (ie Westerners such as myself) to visit former warzones in far-flung corners of the world in organised 'package trips'—a particularly morbid form of tourism. Whilst I'm sure there are those who did so for the best of motives, or at least who would make that claim, it still seemed little more than a bid to experience the imagined 'thrills' of war vicariously, without any concern or acknowledgement of the horrors suffered by those involved. It was also suggested that the practice brought money into areas that desperately needed it—which struck me as a convenient argument to hide behind.

Given the plethora of theme parks that were springing up at the time, I wondered what would happen if officialdom embraced the whole ghoulish concept of warzone tourism and organised a 'fun-filled break' with structured activities in the ruins of such a shattered community. To provide a narrative for the piece, I chose to depict a relationship falling apart, featuring two individuals whose reactions to their visit could not have been more different.

Montpellier

Whilst writing the novel *Pelquin's Comet*, I took my protagonists to the city of Victoria on Brannan's World. Here we caught a glimpse of a very structured and lucrative set-up which helped to generate funds for the criminal organisation known as Saflik. Long after the narrative moved on from the city and the world, I found myself intrigued by what it might be like to live in this place, to perhaps even be one of the cogs that kept the Saflik money-making machine turning. I wrote "Montpellier" to explore this idea. It is a completely stand-alone story, deliberately pitched so that the reader doesn't need to know anything about the Dark Angel novels or even be aware that the story is connected to them in any manner.

The main character, Horner, was an interesting one to write. Cynical, misogynistic, he's a dangerous man, loyal to the criminal interests that have lifted him out of the slums and given him a decent standard of living, but he surprises even himself by the story's conclusion.

No Smoke Without Fire

"No Smoke Without Fire" was not intended to be a story.

Permit me to explain… I never had the opportunity to meet Arthur C. Clarke, though his passing in March 2008 affected me profoundly; both because he was one of the authors I grew up reading and because he was president of the British Science Fiction Association (BSFA), which, at that time, I chaired. I remember sitting in a London pub in the weeks following his death, thinking how wonderful it would be to reprise Sir Arthur's collection *Tales from the White Hart*, to pay homage to a book I loved. As with that classic volume, this would consist of a series of stories involving a recurring cast of characters—scientists, writers, and SF fans—who met regularly in a London pub to share anecdotes, whisper of state secrets, and conjecture about the nature of the universe. The difference being that each story in this new book would be written by a different author.

A while later, I had the opportunity to pitch the idea to my friend, Tom Hunter—head honcho of the Arthur C. Clarke Award—and he loved it. So *Fables from the Fountain* was born.

As this was to be a fundraiser for the Clarke Award, I was able to secure original stories from a host of wonderful authors, including Neil Gaiman, Stephen Baxter, Charles Stross, Liz

Williams, Ian Watson, Eric Brown, James Lovegrove... In order to provide some guidance, I sent each author a cast list of characters' names and occupations—a roster which expanded constantly as more characters were added by various contributors. I also set out to write a few 'guidance scenes' in the pub that would host the gatherings (the Paradise Bar at the Fountain), to provide some context regarding setting, and ensure a uniform 'feel' to the stories.

The problem is that I'm a writer. As I sketched these 'scenes', a narrative started to develop, inevitably becoming a story. "No Smoke Without Fire" resulted, and it ended up being the opening piece of the anthology.

For Your Own Good

Many moons ago, I commissioned a piece of artwork from Hollywood conceptual artist Fangorn (*Eyes Wide Shut, A.I. Artificial Intelligence, War of the Worlds, Corpse Bride, Star Wars, James Bond* etc) for a collection that never happened. Chris (Fangorn) has provided covers for several NewCon titles, which are unfailingly excellent, and this evocative futuristic cityscape is among the best, but it has been sitting on my computer ever since. I love it, but haven't found a suitable project to apply it to. When Francesca at Luna Press approached me with the idea of putting together a short story collection for them, I instantly suggested using Chris' piece on the cover. She loved it too, and the deal was done. The only problem was that none of the prospective stories bore any relation to the cover image, so I set about writing one that did...

Digital Democracy

Back in 2009, Ken MacLeod approached me asking if I could write him a short, short SF piece involving human genetics for 'The Human Genre Project', which he was working on with

Edinburgh University. This all coincided with the expenses scandal that shocked the nation and which so many of our beloved politicians were swept up in. With that in mind, I concocted this alliterative piece for Ken, which he accepted with enthusiasm.

I often employed "Digital Democracy" as an icebreaker at readings, introducing it as the only story I've ever written that takes longer to introduce than it does to recite.

It still is.

Eros for Annabelle

I learnt from a TV programme that the famous statue of Eros in Piccadilly Circus isn't of Eros at all, but of Anteros. For some reason I was amused by this misidentification, and the fact stayed with me, lodged in the hinterbrain. I always knew there was a story in it somewhere, and eventually this resulted in a flash fiction piece set in a post-internet world, which gave me my third appearance in the science journal *Nature*.

Reaper's Rose

There was genuinely a wonderful, evocative scent that haunted me in my younger teens. I've no idea if it was a perfume I smelt once on a passing stranger or something I conjured from my own imagination, but I could evoke it at will and, once I had, it would tantalise me for days. I really did travel into Moorgate on the train every day with my friends for school, and I was once taken to an air show at Duxford by my Aunty Anne (who fed me far too many boiled eggs). This piece required even longer to gestate than "Eros for Annabelle". I've known for decades there was plenty of potential in this memory of a 'ghost scent'; it was just a matter of being patient and waiting for the right story to crystallise. I write very few horror stories, but was quietly pleased with this one, especially when John Joseph Adams accepted it for *Nightmare*.

Beth and Bones

One of the authors whose work I used to devour in my teens was the late great Roger Zelazny. I recall reading (in one of his collections, I think) that, when writing a novel, he would often sketch out a background vignette: something from a character's past never intended to appear in the novel but which the author would know was there, helping to give depth and texture to the character on the page.

When writing my debut novel, *City of Dreams and Nightmare*, I remembered this and decided to try doing the same. In the City of 100 Rows books the city, Thaiburley, is a vital character in its own right, so I opted to write a vignette from Thaiburley's past, set 100 years before the events in the novels. At some point, the vignette took on a life of its own and evolved into a full-blown story. None of the people here recur in the novels, but the setting and many of the accoutrements—street-nicks, the Blade, the Blue Claw—will be familiar to anyone who has read them.

Royal Flush

This is one of the older stories in the collection, having been originally published in 2009. I had the notion to write a mosaic novel about a far future war, in which the conflict itself forms a backdrop rather than the central narrative. The idea was to explore warfare from the perspective of the little people: the foot soldiers who carry out orders oblivious to the rationale, the civilians who endure rather than participate, the mechanics who toil for the cause without knowing whether their efforts make a difference… I've subsequently moved on to various other projects and it's unlikely that novel will ever see the light of day (or indeed, be finished), but several parts of it have appeared over the years as short stories, and this is one of them.

A Triptych for Tomorrow

Flash fiction can be a highly effective vehicle for exploring short, sharp ideas. By portraying your characters convincingly and giving their immediate surroundings texture, while suggesting the wider world via broader references, you can focus on the narrative without the distraction of extensive world building. I wanted to write a series of flash pieces set in the same future, each exploring different aspects of this tomorrow by projecting forward things that are happening in society today, taking them to an extreme (a familiar ambition of much good SF down the years). Each piece stands on its own merit (or at least, so I hope), but they combine to provide a somewhat more comprehensive picture of this near-future world.

The first tale, "Browsing", marked my fourth appearance in *Nature* while the second, "Trending", sold to a completely different venue, *Daily Science Fiction*, so presumably they do stand alone as intended. I wanted to present them here, however, as a single piece, completed by the previously unpublished final story segment, "Temporary Friends", which sees the reappearance of Laura from "Browsing".

The Failsafe

Timing can be so crucial. Sometimes a proposal comes along which, although interesting, is simply made at the wrong time. One such occurred in 2015, when Nathan Hystad invited me to write for *Explorations*, a shared-world SF anthology he was planning via his new imprint Woodbridge Press. I was snowed under with other commitments, so had to decline.

Rarely under such circumstances does opportunity knock again, but on this occasion it did, and in 2017 I was able to write for *Explorations: Colony*, the fourth book in the series. Things had moved on considerably since Nathan first approached me—three previous volumes of stories saw to that—and I was now writing in a future that included the Earth reduced to a cinder, humanity spreading out to the stars, an established political set up, and sentient suns. Well, I'd been intrigued by that last concept ever since I read Frank Herbert's *Whipping Star*...

Sane Day

I set out to do several things with "Sane Day". It concerns me that science fiction can be so clever, so slick, so embracing of technological potentials, that it risks becoming inaccessible to new readers, particularly younger ones. I wanted to see if I could write a story that was pacey, original, with the sort of classic sensibilities that first drew me into the genre. I also wanted to write a story about aliens, with no actual human involvement. The danger in doing so, of course, is that you either anthropomorphise your characters to the point where they aren't alien at all, or you write something so drastically different that a reader can't relate to them... which would undermine the whole idea of making the piece 'accessible'. I compromised. I tried to depict sentience on another world by portraying a society that was distinctly 'other' in its customs and structure while keeping my characters' motivations and reactions within the bounds of the familiar.

I have no idea if I succeeded in any of the above, but I had a lot of fun writing "Sane Day", and here it is in any case.

Between Blood and Bone

This very short piece has an unusual genesis. At the 2017 Eastercon (the National British Science Fiction Convention), I was invited by Tor editor Lee Harris to take part in 'Ready Steady Flash'; four authors (myself, Pat Cadigan, Aliette de Bodard, and Adrian Tchaikovsky), pitted against one another in writing a piece of flash fiction in five minutes in front of a live audience, the themes for each round given to us on the spot by Lee. We then had to read our efforts aloud, with the audience deciding on the best. This was both the most daunting and yet the most fun programme item I've ever taken part in at a convention. Four rounds, four stories (we won a round each, incidentally). One of my pieces was a shambles, two were okay, but I thought the other—written to the theme 'A Change for the Better'—held the kernel of a decent idea. Nearly a year later I revisited the story and wrote "Between Blood and Bone". The setting and actual narrative are very different from the original piece, but the basic concept remains the same.

The Gun

This is another piece written with the vague intention of rolling it up into the mosaic war novel that never happened. It was intended to represent the chaos of war and how easy it must be to become confused; also, how willing a soldier, lost and alone on the battlefield, might be for someone else to take responsibility.

When I was putting together the anthology *Crises and Conflicts* for NewCon Press, I realised that I was one story short, and thought of "The Gun". It was a good fit thematically with the other pieces, and the anthology the story had first featured in was no longer available, so I felt able to include it despite this being a reprint.

I was chuffed when Adrian Tchaikovsky subsequently posted online recommending "The Gun".

The Final Fable

Following the success of the *Fables from the Fountain* anthology, Tom Hunter and I decided to collaborate on a new volume to celebrate the centenary of Arthur C. Clarke's birth (there may have been alcohol involved, ahem). This time, rather than asking contributors to write within a shared world, we would give them free rein to write whatever they wanted; as long as it was SF… and as long as their story was exactly 2001 words long.

We contacted authors associated with the Clarke Award and were delighted by the response. The anthology, *2001: An Odyssey in Words*, features stories from 10 winners of the Award and 13 shortlisted authors, including some of the biggest names in genre fiction (plus non-fiction from former judge Neil Gaiman and three times winner China Miéville).

Partway through the process of putting the book together, Tom asked whether, as a former judge, I was going to write for it myself, confirming that he intended to. This flummoxed me at first. I had a couple of ideas for stories, but none that seemed likely to fit within the very precise word count. Then I remembered the *Fables* anthology; the more I thought about revisiting those characters the more the idea appealed. Earlier in 2017, I'd been one of the speakers at a day-long symposium on the Fermi Paradox, organised by the British Interplanetary Society in London. Other speakers included several eminent scientists and technologists, and some of what I learned there fed into *The Final Fable*. The story flowed remarkably easily and required very little tweaking to fit into the word limit.

This seemed a fitting coda to a cast of characters I'd enjoyed working with and, equally, provides a suitable finale for this collection.

About the Author

Ian Whates lives in a sleepy Cambridgeshire village with his partner, Helen, and a manic cocker spaniel called Bundle. A writer and editor of science fiction, fantasy, and occasionally horror, he is the author of seven novels (four space opera and three urban fantasy with steampunk overtones), the co-author of two more (military SF), has seen some seventy of his short stories published in a variety of venues, and has edited around thirty anthologies. His work has been shortlisted for the Philip K. Dick Award and twice for BSFA Awards. His novel *Pelquin's Comet*, first in the Dark Angels sequence, was an Amazon UK #1 best seller, and his work has been translated into Spanish, German, Hungarian, Czech and Greek. His novella *The Smallest of Things* was published by PS Publishing, October 2018. Ian served a term as a director of SFWA (the Science Fiction Writers of America) and is a director of the BSFA (the British Science Fiction Association) an organisation he chaired for five years. In 2006, Ian founded multiple award-winning independent publisher NewCon Press by accident. www.newconpress.co.uk

Lightning Source UK Ltd.
Milton Keynes UK
UKHW010447040719
345551UK00001B/62/P